HALF
MOON
SUMMER

Published by
PEACHTREE PUBLISHING COMPANY INC.
1700 Chattahoochee Avenue
Atlanta, Georgia 30318-2112
PeachtreeBooks.com

Design and composition by Lily Steele
Edited by Catherine Frank

The illustrations were rendered digitally.

Printed and bound in April 2023 at Lake Book Manufacturing,
Melrose Park, IL, USA.
10 9 8 7 6 5 4 3 2 1
First Edition
ISBN: 978-1-68263-539-1

Cataloging-in-Publication Data is available from
the Library of Congress.

HALF MOON SUMMER

ELAINE VICKERS

Ω

PEACHTREE
ATLANTA

For Jenny

and Elsie
and Addie
and Norah
and Theo

and Kenton

BIRTH DAY
DREW

Every day there are about 385,000 babies born in the world.

Think about it: hundreds of thousands of people with not just your same birthday, but your same Birth Day. When that day started, all 385,000 of you were floating around in the dark, eating and breathing through a cord in your belly, happily swallowing your own pee.

Until it all changed. Until you were pushed from that safe, small, warm world and out into bright lights, cold air, and way too much space, whether you liked it or not.

That's how the big changes happen: *Whether you like it or not.*

I was born in Half Moon Bay, California, on September 23—the very last day of summer that year. I started out like you did, all slimy and grumpy. I screamed like a smoke alarm when Mom tried to feed me and screamed louder when Dad tried to rock me.

Finally, the nurse couldn't take it anymore, so she wedged me into the same bassinet with the other baby who was born that day.

That was the only thing that got me to calm down.

True story.

The next morning, both of us were healthy and ready to go home. Except there was some problem with the paperwork, so it took longer to release us than it should have. Dad sat in the waiting room, pulling his knife across little pieces of wood while the shavings fell like snowflakes into the garbage can. By the time everything was sorted out, he had carved two little birds for the two newborn babies in that bassinet nest.

I've lived in Half Moon Bay ever since, but the other baby left with her family, never to return. Or that's what I thought, anyway.

Pushed from one world to another.

It happened the day we were born, and again the summer before we turned thirteen.

Whether you like it or not.

1
DREW

On the first day of summer vacation, I grab a shovel and head into the fog before the sun's up, looking for buried treasure. Or, okay, not really treasure, but whatever Isaac and I put in the taped-up-shoebox time capsule we buried on the last day of summer vacation last year.

The plan was to dig it up together today and pick up right where we left off. But plans change, so I'm here alone.

Luckily, I'm not totally alone, because I've got my dog, Scout, the greatest golden Lab in history. She runs ahead to check out a gopher hole, then boomerangs back to nudge me along toward the cypress grove.

Even though I don't mean to, I keep wishing I could wind back the clock to *last* summer.

Back before I was old enough (and responsible enough) to babysit my little sister every afternoon.

Back when I hadn't aged out of Little League and when everybody who tried out got a spot on a team somewhere.

Back when my best friend still lived here and I had somebody to hang out with and a hundred fun things to do on any given day, because we could do them together.

I text Isaac, even though he's probably not awake yet.

On my way to the grove to dig up the time capsule
Do you remember where we buried it
Do you remember what's in it
Won't be the same without you

Isaac's family moved to the city last month for his mom's job. After that, everything reminded me of him. I'd pass the hoop where I'd beaten him at a hundred games of H-O-R-S-E and want to challenge him to one more. I'd reach for extra ketchup packets for him on fry-day Friday in the cafeteria. More than once, I waited for him by the flagpole after school until I remembered he wasn't coming.

Isaac's grandparents still live in Half Moon Bay, so he'll still come down every once in a while, but I have no idea how I'm supposed to fill this summer without backyard hoops and gaming marathons and trips to the beach. Summer break has never seemed long enough, but it might seem too long if I have to spend it all alone.

As I wander around the grove, trying to remember where we buried the time capsule, I check my phone, but Isaac hasn't texted back. Maybe he's still asleep. Or maybe he's moved on with city friends who are cooler than me. Maybe the rubber band of our friendship has been stretched too far since he left, and even when he comes to visit and we're finally un-stretched, everything will be not-tight and wrong-shaped. Because, if I'm being honest, he barely even texts anymore.

I have other friends, but they're school friends, or basketball friends. Friends for one specific setting or sport. Isaac was my only anywhere friend, and now it feels like he's nowhere at all.

A bulldog barks at Scout from down the road, and she tries to bark back with the hoarse, high bark her terrible first owners left her with.

"Hey, girl," I say. "Don't worry. We're okay." She pushes her nose against my palm, and I stroke her soft, honey fur: between her ears, over her neck, down her back. We've trained each other, me and Scout.

Then suddenly, Scout stands at attention.

Somebody's coming.

But somebody turns out to just be Dad, rattling through the fog in his old blue truck. He parks and climbs out, thin legs shooting down from basketball shorts like mine, hair cut too close to be as messy as mine.

"Wow, Drew," he says, pulling a bright orange box from the passenger seat and hiding it behind his back like I haven't already seen it. "Fancy meeting you here."

"Fancy as a bologna sandwich."

Dad laughs and ruffles my hair. "Yeah, okay, I came looking for you. Hard to believe you'll be old enough to work in the shop with me next summer."

"Yeah. Hard to believe." At least that part I can agree with. I used to love Dad's shop: the smell of sawdust, the back-and-forth of the guys' jokes and stories. But even though I have zero plans this summer, I'm not sure I'm ready to spend next summer there. All grown up. Working.

"What are you up to this morning?" Dad asks.

"Not much. Just looking for buried treasure."

Dad looks around. "Hmm. By yourself?"

Scout barks again, and Dad laughs. "I didn't mean it. Of course he's got you."

But do I? Scout's already distracted by some other dog's pee on a rock, which seems like a good idea. (Getting distracted. Not peeing on a rock.)

Dad scratches Scout behind her ears. "Find anything?"

"Nah," I say, dropping the shovel in the back of his truck because I don't even know where to dig and I feel kind of embarrassed holding it. "But I think there might be something behind your back?"

Dad swings the box around and holds it out. "There sure is! A surprise for you."

"Oh," I say, kind of surprised. I take the box and flip the lid, and holy cheese nuggets, there they are: black and gray Nikes with bright orange soles and laces. San Francisco Giants colors. The most beautiful shoes I've ever seen. People write songs about shoes like these. They even have a smell—one that says *Nike factory* instead of *knockoff*.

"Try them on," Dad says, even though the solid white seven on the side of the box tells me they'll fit.

When I slide my feet inside, the feeling goes beyond "fit." When I tighten the laces, it's like these shoes were put on this earth to hug my feet.

"Test them out," he says. "Tag that tree and come back."

"Are you sure?" I ask. "I don't think we can take them back if I wear them."

Dad nods and waves me away. So I tag the tree and turn around, and I swear these shoes are like tiny trampolines. When I start to take them off, Dad reaches out to stop me. "What if we take them for a longer test drive?"

"Can't we just shoot hoops?" Dad and I have been playing basketball together since I was old enough to dribble. It wouldn't be the same as playing with Isaac, but it would sure be better than running.

But Dad's not giving up. "I thought maybe we could try something new. Give Scout a chance to run with us?"

"I guess," I say. Maybe we could run past Isaac's grandparents' house, super casual, and just see if his family happens to have come for a surprise visit.

Dad slaps me on the shoulder. "To the pier and back. Last one in the truck has to make breakfast." And he takes off, before I've even thanked him for the greatest shoes I've ever owned. (Or asked him if we can actually afford them.)

We cross Highway 1, then follow the path that winds between the road and the coast, dividing the land from the sea. As we run, Dad starts telling me his whole life story: about his first running shoes, and working in the shop when he was thirteen, and getting his driver's license on the second try after he nearly took out a fire hydrant on his first test.

"Did I ever tell you about the truck I drove, back when I was a teenager? It used to be your grandpa's, and it was a piece of junk. I swear the air conditioner blew hot air. And the thing couldn't even drive in reverse."

We both laugh at that. "Wait, what? How did you get out of parking spaces?" I ask.

"I had to get really creative. Mostly I searched for spots on the curb where I could just drive away after. Either that, or I'd throw it in neutral and have my friends push me backwards. Or a passing stranger. I do not recommend any of this, by the way."

Even with Dad's stories, I swear time stretches and it takes years to get to the old pier. My strategy is just to survive this run and to keep up with Dad, then outsprint him at the end. With these shoes, I'm pretty sure anything's possible.

But when we reach the pier, Dad pulls away and gets there first. Even though this is only the turnaround and not the finish line, I wonder if I need a new strategy.

"Hey," he says. "I might as well give you my breakfast order now. French toast and bacon, please."

Oh, nope. I can't let that happen. So even though I'm still tired and my breathing sounds like double-speed Darth Vader, I shoot into the lead and fight to stay there.

Dad's footsteps beat a steady rhythm behind me and Scout, louder than both of us combined. Every time he gets too close, I speed it up a little, because I'm not losing this thing.

After a while, I realize Dad's breathing matches his steps.

In two, out two.

In two, out two.

So I make my own rhythm, lining up my breath to the steady tempo of my new shoes.

In two, out two.

The fog has all burned off now, and the sun beats down on our backs. I grab the bottom edge of my T-shirt and use it to swipe the sweat from my forehead.

In two, out two.

Scout's quieter as she pads and pants beside me. But I know she's got a rhythm of her own, and it makes me feel like we're doing something wild and free that we were always meant to do.

I can feel my phone in my pocket, slapping against my leg with every other step. Has Isaac texted me back yet? Does he remember where the time capsule is? Does he even remember it at all? Does it matter anyway, if he's not here to open it with me?

In two, out two.

Eventually, I see the hill. The morning has gone 0 percent how I planned it, but when I push up that final rise and slap the back of Dad's truck first, I have to admit it gives me a rush. I try to hang on to that even though something inside me still feels like it's been scooped out.

When Dad comes huffing up the hill, I slap a smile on my face and turn his breakfast order around on him. "French toast and bacon," I say. I'm panting harder than Scout, and then I put my tongue out like hers. Dang, that does feel kind of good.

That's when I notice: Dad's huffing, but not that hard.

"How did you do that?" I ask. "You're not a runner."

Dad smiles. "I used to be. And I'm a runner today." He closes his eyes. "Think of all those years I wasted in between." His breathing's totally back to normal by the time he climbs into the truck.

He didn't let me win, did he?

The question sits in my throat the whole sweaty drive.

Back at home, my quads scream with every one of the twenty stairs between me and our apartment above the woodshop, and I can already tell my pasty skin might be headed for a sunburn. As soon as Luna sees me, she reaches up from her high chair with oatmeal-coated hands. "Out, Dew, out!"

I reach to unbuckle her, but Mom flicks my hands away with her dish towel. "Eww, no."

"It's okay," I say. "I'm not afraid of oatmeal."

"The 'eww' was for you," Mom says. "Can you smell yourself?"

Right then, Dad sneaks in and kisses her on the cheek. She swats him too, but she's smiling. "Both of you, take a shower."

"I owe this kid French toast and bacon," Dad says, opening the fridge.

But Mom grabs him by the shoulders and points him down the hall, then opens the big drawer under the oven and pulls out a frying pan. "Hurry and shower so Drew can have a turn. I'll make breakfast." Which is surprising, because Mom makes pretty decent dinners, but her idea of making breakfast is opening the cereal box for us.

As long as I get bacon, though, I'm not going to argue.

We only have one bathroom, so we've all learned to shower superfast. Dad's clocks in at under five minutes and mine's even quicker. By the time I towel off, suit up (including my new shoes), and open the bathroom door, the smell of breakfast rushes in as the steam rushes out.

In the kitchen, Luna's marching around with an oatmeal beard. The rest of her is cleaned up, though, so I let her sit on my lap instead of strapping her back in the high chair for second breakfast. (Luna eats about eight meals a day right now. Or zero, depending on her mood.) Things are going great until Mom asks the unanswerable question.

"What are you up to today, Drew?"

"Nothing." The word comes out with a sharp edge, and I wish I could take it back and sand it smooth. It's not Mom's fault this summer is going 0 percent how I hoped it would.

Mom glances at Dad, and he gives a little shrug. "I

kind of thought he could keep me company down in the shop after we clean up our mess here."

Great. My last summer before I get swallowed up by the shop and I'm going to start it out . . . in the shop.

But I don't want to hurt Dad's feelings. "I'll come down and draw," I tell him, which is a pretty decent compromise.

"Sounds good to me. Now, who's hungry?" Mom asks, bringing a plate of French toast to the table as Dad flips the bacon.

"Firsty!" Luna says, reaching for my milk, and all three of us say, "Two hands, Luna!"

But it's too late. The milk tips and spills, coating the table and dripping onto the floor.

Mom grabs the dish towel. I scoot my chair back and duck down to help out, but she's just staring at my sneakers.

"Where did you get those?" She's as surprised by the brand-new Nikes as I was, but not in a good way.

Dad clears his throat and grabs the glass, even though it's pretty much empty. "They were on clearance," he says, without looking up at her. "Pretty sweet, huh?"

Mom opens her mouth to say something, but before she makes a sound, the glass clatters from Dad's hand and onto the table, and none of us are quick enough to grab it before it rolls off and falls to the floor. It doesn't shatter, but one crack appears down the side, fast as lightning and shaped like it too.

My parents freeze.

The glass might be ruined, but it's just a glass. Just a little mistake. So why are they both staring at Dad's hand? I take the rag from Mom and start mopping up the milk on the floor.

My best summer ever is officially off to the worst start possible.

Except the second that thought pops into my mind, I wish I could take it back, because I can't shake the feeling that things could be so much worse.

Couldn't they?

2
MIA

INSTEAD

Instead of staying in Sacramento
where we belong,

> my mom
> and my brothers
> and I
> are starting the summer
> with Gram
> in Half Moon Bay.

Instead of being there
with my friends,

> I will be here.
> Friendless.

Instead of busy,
I will be bored.

Instead of spending every day
working side by side with my dad
finishing our new home,

my home
is being split in pieces:
construction site,
storage unit,
Gram's house,
Grandma Jo's.

No more apartment
because
we sold most of what we own
and put the rest in self-store
like a buried treasure
or a time capsule
to open up
when our house is finally finished.

But how can our house ever get finished
if we're not there to finish it?

Until we come back, it will sit,
alone,
a work in progress
without any work
or any progress.

And I'm afraid I will too.

THE WAY TO ALASKA

When Dad told me
Grandma Jo was sick,
I barely believed it.
(She's too tough to get sick.)

And when he told me he was going
to Alaska to help her,
I begged him not to go,
or at least not to be gone long.

We need you here.
We have to finish the house.
Maybe you could just go for a day or two?

Dad shook his head.
You were just a baby last time we went, he says.
So you probably don't remember
how tricky it is to get to Yakutat.

He showed me a map:
white mountain ranges leading to
green inlets and blue ocean
waving and weaving together
like interlaced fingers.

These lines
are the roads.
But what do you notice?

I searched the map
even though I wasn't sure
what I was searching for,
until I realized
what I was searching for
wasn't there at all.

There's no road to Yakutat, I said.

When he nodded, I knew I was right,
even though I didn't want to be.

So how do you get there?
(And, more important, I wondered,
How do you get home?)

On a special plane, Dad said.
Or a ferry, in the summer.
Next time, we'll save up
and take the whole family.
How about that?

I thought of all the other things
we were saving up for:
       a more reliable work truck,
       college for three kids,
       and most of all,
       finishing our house.
And I knew what that meant,
even if nobody was saying it.

It had taken us years just to get one thing
on the saving-up-for list,
and we still didn't have it
quite yet.

It's not so easy to get to Yakutat,
and not only because there's no road.

We wouldn't be going to Alaska together
anytime soon,
so Dad would be going alone.

And none of us even knew
when he'd be coming home.

FIRST PAGE

The night before he left,
Dad told me to write down
everything that happened this summer
in the notebook he gave me
with the silver birds
on the cover.

He didn't tell me why.

But he told me
he would be back from Alaska
before I reached the last page.

He didn't tell me I have to
fill
every
line.
(So I won't.)

He told me long ago
he loved poetry.

I don't.
I like to say what I mean
without dancing around it.

But I do love

white space

filling pages quickly

counting down to the back cover.

So
I decided to write down anything
and maybe even everything
because

he didn't tell me I had to let him read it.

FIRST BIRTHDAY

Grandma Jo and I
have written emails
back and forth
all my life,
but the last few years,
she's been better at the forth
than I've been at the back.

I've only met her in person once,
when I was barely a year old
and too young to remember.

But I've heard the stories,
seen the pictures and videos
so many times
it feels a little like a memory.

After a very long ride on a very big plane
and a very short ride on a very small plane
we found Dad's family right where he had left them—
in a town called Yakutat
at the base of the St. Elias Mountains,
in a house with an orange roof
that Dad helped build before he left for California.

On my first birthday,
that house became the center of my world,
and I became the center of attention.
(I loved that.)

I ate the fried scones Grandma Jo made
with honey and powdered sugar,
licked the sweet stickiness off my fingers
until they gave me another.

(Some kids quit sucking their thumb when they turn one.
That was when I started.)

There's a video of that birthday
I love to watch,
especially now.

Grandma Jo plays a funny little song on the violin,
dipping and swaying
while I sway along with her on Dad's lap.

When she finishes,
she trades with him,
taking me in her arms
and handing Dad the violin.

He holds the instrument up toward the camera—
toward Mom—
with a smile.

Oh boy, she says.
This ought to be good.

He plays a few screechy notes
and Mom laughs—
she has the very best laugh,
clear and bright
like bells on Christmas.

Dad clears his throat,
does some dramatic arm stretches and finger flexes,
and says,
Give me one more chance to impress you.

The camera dips with Mom's nod.

Then

Dad puts the bow to the string
and fills the room
with a melody that sounds
brand-new
and a hundred years old;
like pure joy
and bittersweet sadness,
all at once.

We stayed in Alaska
for two weeks after that,
helping at the café some,
but also
fishing and exploring during the day
with me strapped in a backpack on Dad's back,
singing and eating and telling stories at night.

Every once in a while,
when Dad makes fried scones from Grandma Jo's recipe
or we pass the fish stand at the farmer's market,
I'll wonder if it's impossible
that I actually remember it all.

Because somewhere in my heart,
I swear I do.

SAWDUST

The day we move into Gram's house,
I wear the blue dress she gave me
and unpack my two bags
and two boxes
in about ten minutes.

After that, I am supposed to help the twins,
but they wrestle like puppies
and I'm afraid they will break Gram's breakables.

I think we could all use some air,
Mom says when they tumble off the couch
and land with a crash.
How about a walk?

I nod, and we slip on sandals
and wander down toward the water:
Owen and Oliver
our fearless, four-year-old leaders,
Mom and me trailing behind.

They're so eager to get to the ocean
and Mom is so busy chasing them
that nobody else notices
when we pass a workshop.

The smell of sawdust
and the sound of metal through wood
reminds me so deeply
of Dad
and the house we're supposed to be finishing
together this summer
that I stop walking
so I can breathe it in.
I feel it in my hands too:
sand and saw,
measure and make sure.

Then something in the window
catches the light,
and I step closer to look.

THE VIOLIN

It's not even a whole violin—just

a scroll,   no pegs,
a neck,   no strings,
a body,   no voice.

Still, there's enough that I know
it was a violin once,
and it is waiting
to be one again.

Suddenly, there is a face in the window:
a boy about my age
staring right at me
even though, in the reflection,
it looks like we are standing side by side.

It startles me
and embarrasses me enough
that I rush to catch up with my family.

But in my mind,
I still see a pale part of myself
reflected in the glass—
there with him,
and with the violin.

YOU SHOULD SEE ME

Later,
I take my turn at the computer
to talk to Dad.

When are you coming home?
I ask, hoping the answer will be *Soon*.

But the way he clears his throat
and the way Mom shifts beside me
makes me realize
they've already been talking about this
and I probably won't like the answer.

> *You should see the house here, little bird.*
> *Still as beautiful as ever,*
> *but in need of repairs.*
> *You should see Claire and Naomi, little bird.*
> *Your cousins are*
> *growing bigger and smarter every day,*
> *but they need one more grown-up*
> *now that Grandma Jo is sick*
> *and Aunt Penny has to run the café by herself.*
> *You should see me, running after them.*
> *Remember when Owen and Oliver were younger*
> *and even more wild than they are now?*

I almost say,
You should see ME,
see US.
Don't you see we need you too?

But even in my head,
it sounds selfish.
So I ask again,
hoping this time he'll at least give me an answer.

When are you coming home?

> *We're still figuring that part out,*
> he admits.
> *At least a month, maybe more.*
> *But just think!*
> > *How fun it will be to live with Gram.*
> > *How lucky we moved out of our apartment*
> > *and might be able to save enough*
> > *to finish the house*
> > *since we don't have to pay rent this summer*

How lucky.
How lucky?

Of course I am glad he can help his family.
Our family.
Of course.
But I don't feel lucky.
I feel lonely.

I wonder what my friends are doing
back in Sacramento.
If they are going swimming
and singing karaoke
and training for cross country
without me.

Who am I without them?
Without him?
Without home?

3
DREW

When we've cleaned up the mess and the breakfast, I text Isaac.

Hello? Are you even there??

Then I tuck my phone in my back pocket and go downstairs. Even if I don't exactly have a plan, I'm not sitting around waiting.

If I have to sit around, I might as well be drawing.

Dad's shop was the perfect place to learn to draw, with all its straight lines and rectangles. Once I got good enough at sketching the easy shapes all over the room, Dad scooted my desk under the window to give me a view of cliffs and clouds and my very favorite subject: the ocean. Every day it's different, but every day it's exactly the same. I'm still figuring out how that works.

I watch the gulls over the water and try to capture their

movement, which is hard because, well, they're moving. After a while, the *dring* of Dad's saw stops and he comes up behind me. "Hey," he says, picking up a little wooden bird sitting on the windowsill. "Remember this? I'll never forget that day."

"The day you named me Drew," I say.

He nods. "I guess I should have named you Carver if I wanted you to follow in my footsteps. With a name like Drew, of course you were going to draw."

I wonder if he really is disappointed he didn't name me something else, but I don't ask. Instead, I make a joke. "Ah, yes, I remember that day well."

It works. Dad laughs. Then he looks down at my Nikes. "Hey, you probably shouldn't wear those in the shop. The guy said to save them for running."

I pick up one foot and check out the pattern of the tread in the sawdust. "When am I ever going to run again?"

Dad looks up. "Well, I was thinking maybe tomorrow. We could try a different route, maybe up through town." Does he think it's his turn to make a joke?

But no, he's dead serious.

"Tomorrow?" I ask. "As in, the day that comes after today? As in, run two days in a row?"

"Yeah, and maybe the day after that." Dad lifts one shoulder like it doesn't matter to him, but he looks away too, like maybe it does. "We'll have to start later on days like tomorrow when I have early deliveries, but most days we could go early, like six, before the fog burns off. I was thinking maybe that could be our thing this summer. Now that you finally have some decent shoes for it."

I'm not sure what to say to that. Today's run felt sort of like my yearly visit to the dentist: I'm glad I did it and it wasn't as bad as I thought it'd be, but it's not exactly something I want to do again anytime soon. Definitely not every day. I need an excuse ASAP.

"What about hanging out with friends? You know, social interaction with my peers?"

Dad's face lights up. "Of course your friends can come! Invite them now, if you want."

Well, that wasn't what I meant at all.

Dad's watching me like he thinks I actually have somebody to text. Because last summer, I would have.

"I'll think about it," I mumble as Amarante, Dad's right-hand man in the shop, comes in.

"Drew!" he says, holding out his hand to give me knuckles. "Nice kicks. You a runner now?"

"He sure is," Dad says, before I even have a chance to answer for myself.

"We'll see," I say.

Amarante laughs. "I know better than to get in the middle of that. I'll just grab my instructions and my cabinets and get out of here."

Soon Dad's saw starts up again, and my pencil starts flowing again. Drawing helps me forget that Isaac's gone and I couldn't find the time capsule and when I think about it I'm not even sure we buried it at all and now apparently I have to run every day. It helps a little, anyway.

I finish one sketch, but I need to stretch my legs before I start another, so I stand up and lean against the windowsill.

That's when I see the girl.

She's two steps off the sidewalk, staring up at something in the window next to mine. Tan skin, brown hair, dress as blue as a Dodgers jersey—but I won't hold that against her. Even though she looks about my age, I don't think she goes to my school. So why do I feel like I should know her?

I wave at her through the glass, just to get her attention, but when she sees me, she startles and scrambles away.

Weird.

I wander over to where Dad's lining up a dozen pieces of perfectly planed wood that look like they'll be a headboard by the end of the day.

"Hey," he says. "Can you grab me that clipboard on my desk? I thought I could remember the measurements."

Dad's desk used to be his dad's, and before that it was *his* dad's. It's made from Monterey cypress cut down when they first cleared the main road almost a hundred years ago. The desk has been sitting in the same corner of the shop for longer than either of us has been alive.

Just like the desk, this shop passed from Great-Grandpa Wilbur to Grandpa Herb to my dad (Pete) and someday will come to me, I guess, except my dad named me Drew instead of Carver. But none of them were named Carver, so how come they all knew who they were supposed to be? Okay, they moved from making violins to furniture and cabinets, but all those things feel like a family and drawing is some distant cousin or something. The weird cousin who doesn't belong.

It's a good thing they passed the shop down, though, because we would never be able to afford this place now. Every time we're too poor for travel-team sports or new tires, something in Mom's head says, *A million dollars sure would help*, and then her mouth says it too.

When she says that number—a million dollars—Dad doesn't argue. A million dollars for a tiny rectangle of land and a run-down shop, all because it's by the ocean. But we all know he'll never sell, even if we're driving to rec-league basketball on our old tires. And she wouldn't want him to.

But me? I'd definitely rather have a million dollars than an old shop waiting to swallow me up next summer. Maybe with a million dollars, we could move to the city and live by Isaac again.

But I can't exactly say any of that to either of my parents.

I grab the clipboard and set it on the counter next to Dad. He's one of the best woodworkers in the Bay Area, and he gets commissions from all over the place. From the address on the clipboard, it looks like this one's heading up to Oregon. Dad gives me a little nod, then presses a board against the plate and reaches to bring the saw down on top of it.

But he loses his grip. His hand crashes knuckles-first to the saw table, and for a second, there's not even a thin plastic guard between his fingers and the spinning blade. The board topples and almost falls, but I grab it and straighten it back up. "Holy zombie hands. Want me to show you how to work this thing?"

It's a joke. Another joke. But Dad's face is blank and almost gray, and there's nothing funny about it.

"Hey," he says, powering down the saw. "Let's go back upstairs and get some lunch, huh?"

We had breakfast an hour ago.

Something is weird, so I just nod and follow.

Upstairs, Dad waits until Mom's off her work call, then goes into her office and shuts the door. I'm still trying to understand what's going on. Dad's a perfectionist who is huge on safety—another thing that came straight from Great-Grandpa Wilbur. So how did he lose his grip on the saw? And why did we have an awkward moment over dropping a glass?

If it's not a big deal, why am I sweating? Why does my tongue feel like sandpaper? Why do I want to glue my ear to this door—but also run away?

Down the hall, Luna starts to squawk.

Shhhhh, I whisper as something in me judders.

I listen again, and the second I'm catching a few words—"time to take it seriously"—the juddering comes again, and I realize it's not in me, but on me. My phone is vibrating, not a one-buzz text feeling, but again and again like someone is . . . calling me? I pull it out to silence it, and it's Isaac. ISAAC. He ignores me all morning and then he freaking calls me at the worst possible moment? We NEVER call each other.

I shove the phone back in my pocket and give up on eavesdropping until I can silence both my distractions. When Luna sees me, she squawks even louder and reaches up her little arms for me to lift her out of her crib.

So I pick her up, then lay her down and rip open the diaper tabs. "Luna," I say, trying hard to keep the happy in my voice. "You've created a serious Code Brown here." Luna laughs even though she's two and there's no way she gets the joke, and I could hug her if she wasn't so disgusting right now. Even dealing with a Code Brown is probably better than what's going on in the other room.

But still, I want to know. Sort of. So I hurry to clean Luna up and distract her with toys, then drop the diaper in the pail and squirt some sanitizer on my hands. I'm heading down the hall to try listening in again when the office door opens and Dad comes out. "Drew! Want to head back to the shop?" His voice is every bit as fake happy as mine was with Luna.

I should say yes. Maybe he'd even tell me what's going on. But when Mom comes out of the office and grabs her keys without looking at any of us, I tell myself now might not be the moment. "I'd better stay up here with Luna. Plus, I need to call Isaac back."

Now Mom looks at me suspiciously. "Isaac called you? I didn't think you two ever talked on the phone."

I shrug. "Must be important, I guess. People trust me with the important stuff."

My parents glance at each other. Mom gives Dad a little nod, but he decides to go with the bluff instead. "Of course they do! That's why we trust you to keep our Luna-Lou safe." He scrunches his fingers and lunges like he's going to tickle her, and she shrieks with laughter and buries her head in my shoulder, even though he didn't touch her.

"I'm going into work for a bit," Mom says. "I'll be back in time to make dinner."

"Nah," Dad says. "You made breakfast. Let me take care of dinner." As he kisses her on the side of her head, she closes her eyes and reaches for his hand.

Then Mom's out the door and Dad's right behind, heading for the shop. Luna squirms in my arms, so I let her down, and she disappears down the hallway, leaving me standing at the front window by myself.

Or almost, anyway. Right as I turn away, I see a girl in a blue dress in the distance, walking toward the ocean, and it gives me a flash of a familiar feeling. But not just because I think it's the same girl I saw by the shop earlier.

Weird, I think, as I reach for my phone. When I tip the screen toward me, there's a text from Isaac: *Call me.*

Also weird, I think. He even used a period. But he's my best friend, and I'm curious, so I call him.

Isaac answers after the second ring. "Hey, thanks for calling me back."

"Thanks for texting me back," I say. "Eventually."

Isaac ignores my callout. "Yeah, my parents put text limits on my phone, but this will be better. I have an idea. An epic idea. Have you ever heard of *TitanIAm*?"

"Titanium?" I ask. "Like the metal?" What I really want to ask is *Are we really talking about this when we haven't talked about ANYTHING in FOREVER?* But Isaac doesn't give me a chance.

"No no no no no," he says. Isaac speaks at warp speed when he's excited about something. "With an *I AM* at the end. Like *Titan I Am*, but it's one word. *TitanIAm*. But it sounds like titanium the metal. Now that you mention it, the logo looks like metal, so that's cool, but—"

"Isaac," I say, interrupting him because this could go on for a while. "I have never heard of *TitanIAm*. What is it?"

"It's a new computer game, and it's sick. That's what I was trying to tell you. It's set on Titan, Saturn's largest moon. And you're trying to build colonies and make it awesome. So the name is like the moon but also like somebody who's strong and powerful, so it's like *Titan I Am*. You can build all kinds of structures and cities and you have to find resources and you can play in build mode or survival mode and—"

Is he trying to be my friend again or is he just trying to

sell me some *TitanIAm*? I am so lost that the question that comes out next is, "So it's a *Minecraft* rip-off?"

"NO!" Isaac pauses, and I can almost hear the gears turning in his head as he thinks it over. "Well, okay, maybe, but it is SO MUCH COOLER. The graphics are better, for starters, and it just feels less . . . *Minecrafty*. You want to play?"

"Yeah, I'll check it out sometime."

Pause. "I mean, I thought we could play now, maybe. Like, together? And we could keep talking while we play, so it would kind of be like we're hanging out. You know?"

It still feels like Isaac wants to sell me something, but gaming with him is one of the things I've missed most since he moved. I'm just not sure today's the day to jump into a new world when everything feels so off in this one.

There's no way I can get all that out, so I just say, "I'm supposed to be watching Luna."

"Luna will love it! Plus, it's very educational. It teaches spatial awareness, collaboration, problem-solving, creativity, strategic and critical thinking, and other valuable skills."

"Did you just google 'Why *TitanIAm* is educational'?"

Isaac dodges the question. "Just try it. Ten minutes. Do you really want to spend your summer bored and alone?"

That one stings. "Why are you assuming I don't have any other anywhere friends?"

"I don't know what an anywhere friend is, but I've been out of school since last Wednesday and I am telling you, *TitanIAm* takes care of the bored. And if we talk while we play, it will take care of the alone too. It's a win-win-win-win, because neither one of us is bored and neither one of us is alone! Boom."

"Boom," I say.

"Boom!" Luna shouts as she throws a handful of Cheerios she must have grabbed while I was busy talking. I need to get this kid settled down quick.

"Luna," I say. "Want to watch me play a game?" I put Isaac on speaker, then hurry to search for the app and download it right then. (Luckily, I have money on my account leftover from Christmas.)

"Ten minutes," I tell Isaac as the game loads. "Luna isn't supposed to have much screen time, and we have a Cheerio situation we need to take care of."

Isaac teaches me how to join his world, and it doesn't take too long to figure out the basics of navigation. The graphics are so good I'm already wondering if I might want to do some sketches of stuff we can build together. Isaac keeps a commentary going while we play, and I have to admit, it is kind of like hanging out. I'm not alone. I'm not bored. We've just figured out how to build a bridge across the river so we can get to the masonry resources we need when I hear it.

"Drew? Where are you guys?"

My stomach drops like a lump of granite. Mom's home.

"I gotta go," I say to Isaac, right as Mom opens the door to the office.

Luna and I are both sprawled on the floor in front of my phone, surrounded by the Cheerio boom we never bothered to pick up. How long have we been here?

Mom frowns. "What is this?"

There's no point trying to hide it. "*TitanIAm*," I say, holding up my phone. "It teaches spatial awareness, collaboration, problem-solving, creativity, strategic and critical thinking, and other valuable skills."

Mom is not impressed. "Have you been playing *TitanIAm* all afternoon?"

Luna and I look at each other. "I mean, it took a minute to download . . ."

Mom closes her eyes and takes a deep breath. "Drew, I don't want you stuck to screens all summer. You should be out in the fresh air, or playing your guitar, or both. In fact, that's exactly what you're going to do after you help me make dinner."

So after dinner, I take my guitar out to the deck and start playing. At first, it's just to show that I'm not a terrible son and I do listen after all. But pretty soon, I have to admit it feels great to be out here.

Until Dad comes out and says that Luna is refusing to go to sleep when she knows we are "habbing a potty," which sounds weird unless you speak Luna and know it translates to "having a party."

"Want to go hab your potty on the beach?" Dad asks.

"By myself?" The beach is only a few minutes' walk from our house, but I've never been there on my own after dinner before. (Even though it's totally safe and lots of other kids my age have.)

"Sure," Dad says. "Take your guitar. See if there's anybody you know down there."

"Okay." I toss my guitar in the case and flip the clasps closed before he can change his mind.

By the time I get there, my guitar's a little heavier and the night's a little darker than I'd imagined. But neither of those are bad things, necessarily.

I sit in the sand, facing the waves, and start out with some easy chords. There's a family—parents, grandpa, three kids—roasting marshmallows around a bonfire. They invite me to come over, but I tell them no thanks. I don't move farther away, though. It's okay if they can hear me, and their fire gives me enough light that I can see what I'm doing.

My song ends, and I switch to "Hotel California." One of the dads at the bonfire gives me a whoop and a thumbs-up, so I play a little louder. I'm really getting into it when somebody joins in from behind me.

The voice is high and clear and so close I swear I feel a brush of breath against the back of my neck. I drop the chorus and nearly drop my guitar as I spin around to see where it came from.

Nobody's there.

I glance at the bonfire family, but they're in the totally opposite direction from the voice. I believe in ghosts 0 percent, but I think of the famous ghost of Half

Moon Bay anyway. People around here like to tell tourists about the Blue Lady, who supposedly disappeared back in the 1930s. Some people say she's still here, wailing and breaking bottles and basically haunting the cove. My dad told me that story on this very beach. I didn't totally believe it, but still, I snuggled into my mom's lap just to be safe.

I shake off a shiver and force my fingers to find another song. I haven't played this one in a while, but it's easy enough to remember the chords. It was big a few summers ago, and everybody in Half Moon Bay was obsessed with it because it almost had the name of our town inside.

With our feet in the sand
And our eyes on the sky
The whisper of the wind
As the world spins by

And the waves run blue
'Neath that arc of gold
Where you never grow up
And you never grow old
That's the magic of a half-moon summer

I play the bridge and the chorus, but when it's time for the last verse, I've forgotten the words. Then there it is again: the voice behind me. I'm not the smartest kid in the world—ask any of my teachers—but I don't usually make the same mistake twice. So I keep playing, hoping to lure the Blue Lady (or whoever it is) close enough that I can actually see her.

And it works. Out of the corner of my eye, I see someone standing off to the side. Questions race through my mind, the biggest one being *ARE YOU A FREAKING GHOST?*

The person moves closer, and I see sandals. Legs.

And then—a blue dress.

4
MIA

TONIGHT ON THE BEACH

Some people are scared of the dark,
but darkness makes me brave.
Why be afraid
when nobody can see you?

So
I sit
        by the boy
        on the beach.

I sing
        for the first time
        since Dad left.

I wish
> I could hear his violin
> playing a harmony,
> sliding into perfect thirds
> with my voice.

But he isn't here,
so I sing another song with the boy
instead.

THE BOY

He is
kind blue eyes
hair sticking out in all directions
long legs stretched in the sand
long arms wrapped around the guitar.

I let myself nod and sway and close my eyes
whenever the music asks me to,
just like Grandma Jo did
all those years ago.

I imagine Dad beside me and
something inside my heart
      opens,
            relaxes,
                  releases,
just a little.

Maybe because of the music.
Or maybe because of
the boy.

WHAT WE TALK ABOUT

I love that song,
I say.
When I was little,
I thought there was always a half moon
in Half Moon Bay.

> He laughs,
> says,
> *Seriously?*
> But then he fixes it.
> *I guess I kind of thought*
> *things stayed the same here too.*
> *But they don't.*

I tip my head back
toward the sky
and remember something
Dad taught me once.
The same side of the moon
always faces the earth,
I say.

No matter if you're seeing the moon
from California
or Alaska
or China
or Antarctica,
it's always the same side.

He squints up at the moon.
That's cool.
The moon is cool.
Jupiter and Saturn
have lots of moons
and some of them,
like Titan,
might be able to sustain life.
Then he laughs.
Sorry, that was random.

I laugh with him.
It's okay.
Mine was random too.

Then
we sit quietly
and maybe he,
like me,
is thinking
it's weird
how not-weird it is
to have singing time
and astronomy talk
with a stranger.

How strange it is
that none of this feels strange at all.

What's your name?

Drew.

Do you know any more songs, Drew?

I do, um . . . Gertrude?

I laugh.
Close. My name's Mia.

He rests his chin
on his thumb and forefinger,
fake-serious.
Yeah, that was my next guess.

After that, we take turns choosing songs
until my phone buzzes beside me.

I have to go,
I say
and he nods
like he knows
people don't always get to choose
when to stay
and when
to leave.

THE NEXT MORNING

Funny that it was Gram
who called me home last night
since she is the one
kicking me out this morning.

> *Children should not spend their summers indoors,*
> she tells me
> as she wipes syrup off my brothers' sticky faces.
> *Just text me to check in every hour or so,*
> *and don't go too far.*

I'm grateful,
even if part of me wonders
if she's letting me go
because she's feeling crowded
in her own house.

I almost wear the blue dress again
to thank her for both
the dress
and the freedom.

But I got sand on it last night,
and sand has a way of sticking around.
So I put on shorts, a tank top, and sneakers instead.

Mom is working at her computer,
renewing her real estate license
because she's ready to start working again
now that the twins are old enough for preschool.

She tilts her cheek toward me
and I drop a kiss on it,
then head out,
looking for a way
to fill
       the hour,
            the week,
                 the summer.
To send my roots down a little
into this new soil.

Kamryn and Audrey will start running soon
since we all promised to try cross country.
I try to run by myself,
but I stop after a block,
not because it's too hard or I'm too hot
but because it feels
so lonely.

So I walk instead,
wandering toward town
with no real purpose
until I find my way to the tiny hospital.
The place where I was born.

Is Dad sitting with Grandma Jo
right now
at another hospital
two thousand miles away?

RUNNERS

When I find the hospital,
I follow the path up to the building,
rest my hand against the cool brick.
Voices drift toward me, and when I turn
it's not doctors or nurses but
two runners.
One taller
and one shorter,
a father and son
with a dog padding along beside them.

Once they've passed, I can't help it.
I follow them.

I follow them because
the son looks like
the boy from the beach
and because
I wish that
instead of running after my cousins,
my dad was here,
running with me.
(Even though we have never gone running together before.)

FINISH LINE, STARTING LINE

We wind out of town and toward the coast
until finally the father and son find their finish line:
a lemon tree in front of a woodshop.

They laugh,
stopping to sit on the stairs that lead to a door one story up
as a little girl comes out the door and turns around,
lowering herself down with her belly on each step.

When she reaches the bottom, the man scoops her up,
cradling her so perfectly in his arms that I ache a little.
The boy goes inside, but the man stays,
looks toward the water.

Toward me too.
Then I hear his voice.

You coming again tomorrow?

I glance over my shoulder, but nobody's there.
He is talking to me.

Am I coming again tomorrow?

The little girl puts her hands on her dad's cheeks,
turns his head to see what she sees in the ocean.
He whispers something in her ear that makes her giggle.

But then he looks back at me.
He hasn't forgotten.
He is a dad,
a good one,
and he hasn't forgotten me.

Okay, I say.

He smiles.
We're starting earlier.
Six o'clock, under the lemon tree.

I nod.
I'll be there.

After they've gone inside, I sneak closer
and suddenly
I realize
I've been here before.

I didn't recognize the shop at first
because there's no sound of saws,
no smell of sawdust,
and because I've only seen it
from the other side.

But even before I round the corner,
I know the violin will be there.

The boy I followed on the run
is also
the boy I sang with on the beach
and
the boy who startled me in this window
just yesterday.

Drew.

What are the odds that I would see the same person
in three different ways
in less than a day?

Much bigger in this small town
than in Sacramento, I admit.

But still.
But still.
Could it be
that the universe
is trying to tell me something?

ON MY OWN AGAIN

I stay close to the coast,
smelling the sea and citrus,
listening to the cry of the foghorn
until the sky turns blue again,
watching from the top of the cliffs
as the seals savor the warmth.

In Sacramento, summers are too hot
to do anything but try to escape the sun.
But here, the sea keeps things so much cooler
I can't blame the seals for their basking.

I text Kamryn and Audrey
to tell them I might be running here this summer,
then explore the library—
the crayon-bright children's section,
the plaques and pictures of local history.

One plaque tells about a missing person people call
the Blue Lady
who disappeared almost a hundred years ago
and how people still imagine they
  see her near the cliffs
  hear her wailing
  find the bottles she's broken in the night.

I think of me in my blue dress yesterday,
a ghost of the girl I thought I'd be this summer,
and maybe I know
just a little
how it feels to disappear from
your own life.

BELONG

When Gram comes to say good night,
she sits beside me on my bed,
holding something small between her hands.

> *I still remember the day you were born,*
> she says.
> *There was another baby born here*
> *the very same day.*
> *A little boy*
> *with quite a set of lungs*
> *and quite a set of eyelashes.*
>
> *His father sat there*
> *with a pocketknife and a piece of wood,*
> *and the next thing I knew,*
> *he was handing me this.*

Gram lifts her fingers,
and there in the nest of her palm
is a little wooden bird
peering up at me.

> *I think it's a sandpiper.*
> *I've kept it on a little shelf*
> *all these years*
> *to remind me of that day.*

I'm embarrassed to say
I didn't realize
that it wasn't meant for me.
He made it for you.
Look.

She turns the bird over to show me
my name carved on the bottom.

Gram pulls me close.
You belong here, Mia.

I start to lean away,
but Gram's arms are stronger than they look.

I know, I know.
You belong in your own home and with your
dad even more.
But I don't want you to feel for one moment
that you don't have a place here.
You always have.

She leaves the little wooden bird
on my nightstand
and I am glad that
at least one of us is where she belongs.

REFUGE

If I could fly,
I would leave this place
and fly to Sacramento
and the life I left behind.

I would fly to Alaska
to visit Dad
and Grandma Jo.

I touch the carved bird's wings with my fingertips,
and a memory comes back to me:

I am seven years old,
visiting a wildlife refuge with my dad,
watching thousands of birds
      northern pintails and
      tundra swans
flying north for the summer.

Some land gracefully on the water
and others fly on,
but they all seem to know
just what to do.

I slip my hand into his,
filled with wonder,
and with questions.

I ask them all,
partly because I want to know,
and partly because I want to make
the moment
last
as
long
as
I
can.

How do they know when it's time to leave?
How do they know where to go,
and how to get back?
How do they know when it's time to come home?
How do they know where home is?

Now, alone in my bed,
I wish
I could remember
any of the answers he gave me.

But I am not alone for long.
A few minutes later, the twins sneak in,
curling up beside me—
Owen on the left, Oliver on the right—
warm and wiggly as puppies.
I smooth their hair,
kiss their puppy noses.
They squirm and smile,
then drift back to sleep beside me.

And I wonder
if I can find refuge here—
      at least a little,
      at least for now?

BRAVE ENOUGH

When my alarm chirps,
Owen and Oliver are still there,
warm and dreaming,
and it is still dark.

I am brave enough
to slide out from between them,
hurry to the woodshop,
and wait.

The dog smells me,
sees me,
circles me once,
nudges my hand with her nose,
gives me the courage
to step out of the shadows.

Okay, I tell her.
I'm ready.

5
DREW

When my alarm blasts me awake at 5:55 a.m., I stumble out of bed and don't even look in a mirror or put on deodorant because it's just supposed to be me and Dad in the half dark and who cares and then PABAM! I trip down the last stair because there's a girl leaning against the lemon tree.

It's not just any girl, though. I'm pretty sure it's Mia, the blue-dress girl from the beach, who is maybe the same girl I saw outside the shop.

I am not the smoothest with girls. Somehow it wasn't awkward on the beach, but holy cheese nuggets, it's awkward today.

Dad sticks out his hand to shake hers. "Glad you made it! I'm Pete."

Glad you made it? I wonder. *Did Dad invite her here?* Then I realize I've been staring at the girl like a creeper and my dad is also smoother with girls than I am.

"I'm Mia," she says.

So it's definitely her. Is she stalking me? Is she the Blue Lady?

Dad stretches his calves. "Good to meet you, Mia. We'll probably go a little bit past the pier today."

"Sounds good," Mia says.

And just like that, we're off.

We don't really say much. Not sure why Mia's quiet, but for me, it's because we're going faster than yesterday. I'm trying to stay as far ahead of Dad as I can (but also not pass out), plus I'm wondering if my in two, out two breathing is weird, and also, how many places can the human body possibly produce sweat from anyway?

When we get to the pier, I turn to ask Dad just how much farther we're going.

Only he's not there.

"Dad?" I ask.

"He fell back a while ago," Mia says. "He told us to keep going."

I look for him way down the path, but no luck. Even though the air's clear, something feels foggy. "I heard him say to keep going, but he always says that, and usually he keeps going too. At least we can head back now."

I start to turn toward Dad (and home), but Mia doesn't follow. "He said to go past the pier. Aren't you going to go past the pier?"

"Oh, sure." I run four whole steps past the pier. "Now we're turning around."

But she runs to me plus a few steps farther.

So I run past her, then she runs past me, again and again. Pretty soon we're slingshotting past each other over and over and around the corner. I can't even see the pier anymore. Finally, we look at each other, both of us sweaty and stubborn, and burst out laughing.

"We should probably turn back now," she says, like she could run a hundred more miles.

"Yeah, if you're tired," I say, and I take off.

When we're halfway home, I finally see Dad up ahead—limping. Scout's circling him, acting nervous. "Holy cheese nuggets." Mia snickers at me until she sees where I'm looking.

At first, it's hard to tell how bad Dad's hurt, but when we catch up, there's blood trailing down his leg and soaking into his sock. I just stand there, wondering why I feel off-balance too, as Mia darts under his arm like a human crutch.

"What happened?" I ask.

He tries to smile. "Took a tumble. Did you go past the pier?"

"Way past," Mia says. Some of the pain disappears from Dad's eyes when she says it. Then I'm glad we kept going, even if it's weird for that to be so important to him right now.

"Why didn't you yell at us to stop?" I ask.

Dad waves the words away. "I'm fine. Plus, I had my loyal canine companion with me."

Scout looks up even though nobody said her name. I kneel down and wrap my arms around her. "You are the best dog in the whole world," I murmur into her fur. "You know that, right?"

Dad hobbles forward. "Help me up to that parking lot," he says. "Your mom should be here any minute."

So I become the other human crutch. We shuffle over to the parking lot just in time for Mom to show up with water and bandages and baby wipes for the blood. When he's all cleaned up, Dad gives Mom a sweaty kiss and says, "Thanks. See you at home."

He starts limp-running down the trail. Mom stands there for a second with her mouth open. "Are you serious?" she calls. "I can drive you home." She looks like she's about to take off after him, but then he gives her a wave over his shoulder and Luna starts crying in the back seat.

Mom turns to me, and she is not messing around. "Stay close to him. Call me if I need to come get you guys."

Mia grabs my elbow and leads me toward the trail. "We will," she says. "We promise."

It only takes us half a minute to catch Dad with his messed-up stride. I expect him to be in pain, but he's smiling.

"What a lucky thing to be able to do this," he says. "Do you know how many systems in my body are already ramping up, constricting vessels and releasing clotting factors and doing everything else it takes to fix my scraped knee?" He looks down like his leg might be healed already or something. Then he smiles at us, bigger than before.

"Do you know how much is happening inside all three of us right now—chemical and electrical and mechanical—so that we can run down this path? It's like a symphony of a thousand instruments, each playing its part perfectly while your brain conducts the whole thing." Dad throws his arms in the air and shouts to the sky: "Our bodies are amazing!"

This is maybe the most embarrassing moment of my life. It feels like Health Class: Dad Edition. For once, I'm glad my face gets red when I run so it won't be obvious I'm blushing. Who knows what's going to come out of his mouth next?

Maybe I should talk instead. "Anyway . . ." I say. My mind is blank. I can barely remember my own name. Name! That's a normal thing to ask about! I turn to Mia. "What's your last name?"

"Fisher," she says. "Mia Fisher."

Dad claps his hands. "Hey now! Are you serious?"

Even Mia's surprised by that one. "Do you know my family or something?"

He nods. "And you two know each other. But I'll let you figure out how."

"Because we met on the beach when I was habbing a potty?" I ask.

Dad laughs. "Nah, you go back farther than that. What an amazing day! Hey Mia, does your grandma still have that bench I made her?"

Mia looks over at Dad. "No. I mean, I don't know." She bites her lip. "Um, you're bleeding through your Band-Aids."

Dad shrugs. He doesn't even look down. "This sock is done anyway. You're a miracle, Mia Fisher," he says. "And so is this son of mine. I mean, look at you two!"

There's really no way to follow that up, so we run in awkward, sweaty, amazing-body silence until we get to the lemon tree.

After Mia's gone, Dad grips the railing as he powers up the stairs, two at a time. I'm trying to figure out a way to inform Mom that he's lost it, but when we come through the door, I can tell she already knows.

"Today," she says. She's staring straight at him. "There was a cancellation, so they can fit us in if we come today. Amarante and Tony are covering the shop, and my sister is coming to stay with the kids."

"Oh, *today*," Dad says. He takes a deep breath before he locks into her laser eyes. "Okay then. Today it is."

"What's today?" I ask.

Dad thinks for half a blink, then pastes his smile back on. "Your mom has a work conference in the city I promised I'd go to. We thought it had filled up, but I guess there's an opening. I didn't even realize it started today. Will you help out with Luna?"

Mom wheels a suitcase right past us and out the front door. She hates conferences, and she is definitely not wearing work clothes. Everything is weird and wrong and I'm not even sure what questions to ask.

So I just spit one out.

"When will you be back?"

"Oh, it's only a couple of days," Dad says. I wonder how he knows when he didn't even remember this thing was happening. "Hey, promise me something."

I nod.

"Promise you'll run in the morning. Farther than today."

"Okay."

Outside, Mom revs the engine, but I can't let him leave with everything this weird. I need to make him laugh.

"Because my body is amazing?"

He hugs me hard. "Damn right it is."

Dad doesn't swear. Ever.

He pulls away and looks me straight in the face. "Run with Mia if she shows up. You two really should get to know each other. But even if she's not there, you run for me, okay?"

"Okay," I say. I'm too freaked out about what's going on with him to spend more than a second wondering what he means about Mia. He wraps one arm around me and the other around Luna and holds us for a long time, and then he's gone.

A few minutes later, Aunt Shannon shows up with

toys and books to keep Luna busy and movie ideas and microwave popcorn for tonight. After that, I hear Tony firing things up in the shop downstairs. It does feel like my parents could be at a work conference.

Maybe all the weirdness is in my imagination. Maybe Dad was just acting strange this morning because he knew he was forgetting something. Maybe he just fell because sometimes that happens.

Maybe this can still be the best summer ever and everything will stop falling apart around me.

For the rest of the day, I escape to *TitanIAm* with Isaac, and every time my thoughts come back to earth, I try to convince myself all my maybes could be true.

Sometimes, it even works.

The next morning, my "amazing" body is wide awake at 5:55 again, even without the alarm clock. As soon as Scout sees me roll over, she runs to the window and noses under the curtain. I rub the sleep out of my eyes and peek through with her.

In the distance, the ocean churns and sprays, but our street is pretty calm. A few puddles shine in our tiny parking lot, pinpricked by rain.

Rain is a good excuse. I can just climb back into my bed because it's probably not a good idea to run in the rain. Right?

Then I notice Mia, standing under a tree and staring up in our direction.

I drop to the floor. "Maybe she didn't see us."

Scout shifts to get a better look, and the curtains shift too. Her tail wags.

"Hey, stop that. Get down."

Scout barks her hoarse bark. She runs to my bedroom door and waits for me to let her out.

Apparently Scout and Mia are going to make me keep my promise.

Fine. I leave a note for Aunt Shannon, then head out the door.

Mia smiles when she sees me.

"For a second I thought you were hiding up there."

"Oh, I was," I say. "But Scout's terrible at that game."

"Where's your dad?"

"At a work thing for my mom." If it's a lie, he probably meant it for both me and Mia. "He said to go without him."

Mia tightens her ponytail. "Did he say how far?"

"Farther than yesterday, if you can handle it."

She stretches her calf against the curb, just like Dad. "Oh, I can handle it. But if you get tired, we can always turn around." She's wearing purple running shorts and a gray tank top, and I'm willing to bet those aren't the clothes she slept in. My own T-shirt itches against my skin.

Did I ever change after we ran yesterday?

Have I been wearing these clothes for a solid thirty-six hours?

Does she remember I wore this yesterday?

Can she smell me from there?

Why isn't it raining at all anymore?

Could I fake an injury to get out of this?

Too late now.

I'm alone with this girl and our amazing bodies.

I tighten my laces. "Well, let's get this over with."

Once we're running, we joke around, mostly about YouTubers we like and the weird things our little siblings say. Before I know it, we're back at our house. Mia taps the lemon tree like it's a finish line, then heads home with a wave and a quick goodbye. I was worried she was going to ask more about Dad, but she didn't.

Is she just respecting our privacy, or does this all seem normal to her? Should it seem normal to me too?

Dad and Mom come home the next afternoon, acting like everything is fine. They tell me they've done some research on *TitanIAm* (when?) and talked to Isaac's parents, and we're allowed to keep playing together, as long as we also call each other and talk about other stuff too so we can have "actual human interaction."

Mia keeps showing up every morning, so the three of us keep running, and my in two, out two breathing starts to sound less like Darth Vader. One day, Dad says Mia should bring her dad too, and she tells him her dad is out of town in a way that seems so sad around the edges I know there's got to be a story behind it. But she doesn't tell it, and I don't ask.

Another day, Mia gives me her phone number. It's weird how not-weird it is.

The next day, she texts me to see if I want to go down to the beach that night. My parents say yes (because "actual human interaction"), so we go, and the beach is awesome. Something about the salt air or the sound of the surf makes it easier to talk about the real stuff, I guess, because Mia tells me about her dad and shows me pictures he's sent from Alaska and the house they're building together back in Sacramento. (That makes me feel a little guilty, since I'm trying to avoid working with my dad when all she wants is to be working with hers.)

After that, the days fall into even more of a pattern: running early with Dad and Mia, *TitanIAm* with Isaac right after lunch, Luna and chores for the rest of the afternoon, and meeting Mia in the half hollow by the beach after dinner. It's almost enough, except I still miss the "actual human interaction" of hanging out with Isaac in person, and now that I've noticed it, I can't unsee the sadness along the edges of Mia.

One day, near the end of a run, I finally remember to ask her what she was doing outside the shop window the first day I saw her. When she tells me she was looking at the old violin and how her dad plays beautifully but doesn't actually own a violin, I know exactly how to make the sadness go away, just for a minute.

So I do.

I take her into the shop and tell her it's all hers.

"You can fix it up and learn to play too," I say. "We can give a concert. Or be buskers."

"Buskers?"

"Yeah, people who play for money, like in parks and street corners and stuff."

"That can't possibly be the name for it."

"It is! They have buskers in *TitanIAm*." (They do. Don't ask.)

"That's the word they use in your game, so it must be correct? Drew, I know you've sold your parents on *TitanIAm* being educational, but . . ." Mia laughs, then looks down at the violin. "Maybe my dad and I could fix it up together when we get back. When we're done with the house."

"That's a great idea," I say. "And we could still give a concert, you could just sing instead. Unless you're afraid I'll kick your busk at that just like I do at running."

Mia rolls her eyes, but then she's back to examining the violin. I can tell she's excited about it, and it feels good to fix something myself, even if it's just fixed for now. An image flickers at the edge of my memory. Did Isaac and I make up a superhero like that, once upon a time? Fixer Man or something? Is that part of what's in the time capsule I still haven't found? (Or, okay, even looked for that much.) I'll have to ask him.

Mia sets the violin down and gives me a giant hug before she goes.

"See you tonight!" she says, and even though we ran five miles today, she's practically running down the street, and she looks like she might float away, lunar gravity–style.

I am a good friend, I tell myself, the warmth of it filling me up.

At least I've got that going for me.

6
MIA

LINES IN THE SAND: PART 1

busker [buhs-ker] (noun): someone who performs on the street or in a public place, especially for money

I can't believe Drew was right.
It sounds like such a made-up word.

After dinner,
I hurry to the beach
to tell him so.

But Drew isn't there.

I wait for him,
wishing I hadn't forgotten my phone,
until
I am tired of waiting.

So I take a stick
and walk down toward the water,
where the beach is wet enough that
the lines I draw will stay
and I write my wish
into the sand.

I WANT TO GO HOME

Nothing happens.
Except,
maybe not nothing.
Another memory,
of lines drawn
not in the sand,
but in the dirt.

The beginning
of home.

THE BEGINNING OF HOME

On my tenth birthday,
Dad was so excited to show me my present
I wasn't sure how his feet were even staying on the ground.
He brought me to the truck and handed me a blindfold.
Are Mom and the boys coming? I asked.

Not today, he said. *Today is just for you.*

I was glad to get out of the apartment because
as Owen and Oliver and I grew bigger and bigger,
our apartment felt smaller and smaller,
especially the tiny bedroom
my brothers and I shared.

It took five songs on the radio to get to where we were going,
and when Dad turned off the engine,
I could hear kids laughing nearby,
and below that,
the steady *brum* of a lawn mower.

Dad opened my door,
took my hands as I stepped out of the car,
turned my shoulders just a little
and counted down.

3 . . . 2 . . . 1 . . .

When the blindfold disappeared,
I blinked myself back into the world.

Oh, I said,
staring at the rectangle of dirt in front of me.
I searched for something else to say,
but all I could come up with was,
Wow.

> *I know, right?*
> Dad stood out in front of me.
> *Can you even believe it?*

I looked
left

           and

                    right

where actual houses stood
shading actual yards.

Then I glanced down and saw:
it wasn't just a rectangle of dirt.
There were rectangles spray-painted *in* the dirt.

Rectangles the size of rooms,
the soil inside them raked so smooth
it looked like just-vacuumed carpet.

Even though Dad and his crew
had framed a hundred houses or more,
we'd never had one of our own.

Is this our dirt?
I barely dared wish it.
Are we building a house here?

   He nodded.
   All those years building houses for other families,
   and now I finally get to build one for you.

I looked over our little piece of land.
Are you sure we can afford it?

   He gave my hand a squeeze.
   Yup. It'll take a couple of years, since
   I'll have to do a lot of the work myself
   and trade labor for the jobs I can't do.

Right then, it was hard for me to imagine
anything
my dad couldn't do.

> *We can do some of the work together,*
> he said,
> *if you want.*

Across the street, weeds sprouted
through all the cracks in the sidewalk.
But there were none on our property.
Already, Dad loved and cared for this place.

> He guided me by the shoulders
> to the first line in the dirt.
> *Let's just open the front door,*
> he said, reaching out
> and turning the imaginary knob.
> *I'll show you around.*

> In the kitchen,
> Dad pretended to light birthday candles.
> In the living room,
> he showed me the little alcove
> where Gram's piano would go.
> *She always wanted us to have it*
> *when we got a house of our own.*

Down the hall,
he showed me the bathroom
and the room he and Mom would share,
then opened another imaginary door
into a smaller rectangle.
This is Owen and Oliver's room.
Isn't that fantastic?

For a second, I wondered
what was so fantastic about it,
but then I realized what that meant.

Hope bloomed in my belly.
It's their room, but not mine?

That's right.
Dad smiled, and we stepped inside
one last rectangle.
This is your room, little bird.
He drew two notches
in the line of the wall.
And your very own window
for wishing on stars
all the days it's not your birthday.

Beyond my window,
a branch from the neighbor's tree
reached over the fence
as if it were handing me an apple,
welcoming me to the neighborhood.

Thank you, I whispered,
to the apple tree
and the rectangle in the dirt
and most of all,
to my dad.

LINES IN THE SAND: PART 2

Now, as the sun sets over the ocean,
I try to remember
where to put all the rooms
of our almost-finished house.

Does the porch stretch all the way across the front,
or is that only at Grandma Jo's house?
Do I share a wall with my brothers,
or is the bathroom between us?
How did Dad make it
all fit together
so
perfectly?

Back in Sacramento,
our house only needs carpet
and a few finishes and fixtures
before we can move in
after all this time.

If Grandma Jo hadn't gotten sick
and Dad hadn't left for Alaska
we might be living there already.

But now, here,
it is slipping away from me,
and soon the tide will erase all my lines
into smooth sand anyway.

7
DREW

It turns out, I'm kind of a terrible friend—but tonight, that's the only way to be a good son. Because even though I'm supposed to be at the beach already, somehow I'm standing in my kitchen instead, offering to babysit.

"I know you were planning on going to the beach," Mom says. "And we've never made you do Luna's bedtime routine before. Are you sure this is okay?"

Well, I mean, no. I'm not sure. But I can't tell her that I think going down to the beach for the billionth night in a row is more important than staying home with Luna so she and Dad can go to dinner and use the fancy theater tickets that have been on the fridge for the last two weeks. When Aunt Shannon had to cancel, I knew what the answer had to be before Mom had finished asking the question, even if I'm 99 percent sure I won't perform the bedtime routine up to Luna's standards.

"Of course," I say. "I'll just text Mia and tell her. We

can go tomorrow night. It will be fine. You and Dad should go and have fun."

They should, but they won't. Something's different since they got back from the "work conference" in the city. Even more different, I mean.

So they go, and I stay, and I text Mia, but she doesn't answer.

Luna says she doesn't need a bath, and even though I'm pretty sure she does, I let it go. We eat popcorn and yogurt and then I brush her tiny teeth and grab a stack of picture books—throwback favorites from when I was little. I toss an extra pillow onto her bed like Mom and Dad do when they read her bedtime stories.

"I'll keep reading until you fall asleep, okay?"

Luna snuggles up next to me. "Okay, Dew."

As I'm reading, I keep telling myself that as soon as she's out, I'll see if Isaac can play *TitanIAm*. That having the house to myself will be kind of awesome.

But Luna falls asleep on my sleeve and I don't dare move. Or maybe I don't want to. Across the hall, my parents' room is so dark and empty, and all I want is to stay here with Luna in this tiny bed and wake to their voices speaking soft and low, telling me it's okay, leading me down the hall and tucking me into my own bed, the covers cool on my skin. I want Mom to kiss my forehead while Dad squeezes my toes, in that way that makes me feel safe, top to bottom.

Is that really what they used to do? I wonder. Everything

has changed so much in the present that even the past feels changed too.

So I keep reading—silently, to myself—these books I remember from my childhood. Of course I know I can't be a little kid again, and I don't want to be. But there's something nice about already knowing all these stories will have happy endings, and knowing exactly what the endings will be. I wish I knew what was coming after the next page turn in my life.

Except, kind of, I don't.

8
MIA

APOLOGY

When I get home,
there are three texts from Drew,
apologizing that he can't come after all.
I tell him I understand,
and I do.

The next morning, we run,
and things are back to normal—
or almost,
anyway.

Even though it's my fault
for forgetting my phone
and definitely not Drew's fault that
he had to help his parents,
it still hurts
when somebody
doesn't
show
up.

IMPORTANT PAPERS: PART 1

After my run, I take Owen and Oliver to the park
and teach them the slide monster game that
Drew and Luna play.
(My brothers love it.)

When we get back,
Mom is in her room,
digging through the box of Important Papers
we brought from Sacramento.

What's up? I ask.

> She jumps back like
> there was a snake in the box.
> *Mia. Hi. Just looking for something.*

For what?

She closes her eyes
like this is a really hard question
even though she must have known
what she was looking for.

Finally, her eyes meet mine,
the pain on her face catching me by surprise.
> *For the loan paperwork on the house.*

This house?
Or our house?

> *Our house,* she says.
> She chews on the corner of her thumbnail
> and won't look me in the eye.
> *It looks like we're going to have to sell it.*

My mind scrambles to make sense of this.
The house is almost finished.
We're supposed to move in before school starts.
We're finally going to have a house of our own.
Except maybe we're not.
Why?

> Mom sets the folder down,
> puts her hand to my cheek.
> *It was always a stretch,*
> *and now we've gotten behind on payments.*
> *We want to give you the world, Mia.*
> *That's why we put every extra dollar*
> *and Dad put every extra minute*
> *into the house for so long.*
> *But all the time he's spent on the house*
> *is time he hasn't been doing paid work.*

Guilt snaps and pricks inside me.
How many times have I asked Dad when the house would
be ready?
How many times have I begged him to hurry?

> Mom finds the folders she's looking for
> and pulls them from the box.
> *It's just a house,* she says,
> but the way her voice catches on the words,
> I know she doesn't believe them either.
> *Home is where we are together.*

That's the problem.
There's NOWHERE we are together right now.

IMPORTANT PAPERS: PART 2

Where will we live?

Finally, Mom looks me in the eye,
but it's like she's got her guard up now
to protect me.
Or maybe to protect her.

It's looking like we'll live here
longer than we thought.
I'll work,
and we'll save up,
and we'll go back when we can.
But you'll be starting the school year
in Half Moon Bay.

What about my friends?
My life?
I look around the little bedroom
that Mom's been staying in.
Where will Dad even sleep
when he comes back?

Dad will go to Sacramento
and get back to his business.
Somebody on his crew
has an apartment above his garage
Dad can stay in for free
until we save up
and figure something out.

Can I stay there too?
Then I could still—

No, honey, I'm sorry.
The apartment's only big enough for one person.

So even when he comes back,
we won't be together?

Mom doesn't answer,
but her silence is answer enough.

Can't we do anything?

There's nothing else we can do.
It's not up to us anymore.

Who's it up to?

Mom's eyes flicker to the folders in her hand.
That's complicated, she says at last.
She keeps one of the folders
and shoves the other back in the box.

And then she's gone.

I pull out the folder she left behind and flip it open,
but it's just a bunch of papers
with a bunch of numbers on them
and some guy's name at the top
with a red sticker on the tab
and none of it makes any sense to me.

None of this makes any sense to me.

YOU'LL NEVER WALK ALONE

After dinner, I sit down at the old piano,
trying not to remember that
this piano was almost ours,
trying not to picture
how perfectly it would have fit
in the alcove Dad built for it
      in the house
            that isn't really ours anymore.

The floor creaks.
Gram.

      She smiles like she knows a secret.
      Runs a dustrag over the top of the piano.
      Did you have fun at the beach last night?

My cheeks burn,
but she just laughs.
I slide over, and she sits next to me
on the piano bench.

I don't sleep so well anymore,
so I've heard you leave at night
and in the mornings too.
It seems like maybe you don't sleep so well anymore eith

It's not a question,
but I nod in answer anyway.

How's your dad doing?
And your grandma Jo?

I shrug.
Okay, I guess.

I only went to that café of hers once,
back when your parents were first married,
Gram says, running her fingers over the piano key
with a dreamy look in her eyes.
But I swear I can still taste those scones.

Gram begins playing
an old Broadway song I love,
the notes
soaring
and falling
and seeping under my skin.
Her fingers don't seem old at all when she plays.

Oliver and Owen come listen in the doorway,
but they scurry away, giggling, when Gram looks at them.

I release my fingers
one   by   one
from this bench
that doesn't quite match its piano
and a memory
pulls loose from my mind.

Gram, where did you get this bench?

> She smiles.
> *Well, that's a story*
> *I should have told you by now.*
> *Remember that little wooden bird*
> *I gave you when you moved in?*

From the day I was born?

> Gram's fingers find one of the curves
> carved into the corners.
> *That's right.*
> *Well, a year or two later,*
> *the old bench I'd sat on with my own mother*
> *finally gave out.*

I had planned to go
to the piano superstore in the city,
thinking I wanted something
fancy and adjustable
and softer for my backside.
A bench for one,
since it was just me at home.
But as soon as I set out
down Highway 1,
I saw the man out in front of a woodshop:
the one who carved those birds.
I stopped,
and we got to talking,
and the next thing I knew,
we were sketching the piano bench
he was going to build me.
I can't even recall his name now.

The name tumbles from my mouth,
as uncertain and hopeful as a little bird.
Was it Pete?

Her face brightens.
Yes, I believe that's right.
How did you . . .

A timer goes off in the kitchen,
and I'm left
alone
to realize the rest of what that means.

You go back farther than that,
Pete had said about me and Drew.

I had no idea he meant
all the way back
to the beginning.

DUET: PART 1

That night,
on my screen,
I tell Dad about Drew and Pete,
show him my little wooden sandpiper,
ask if there are sandpipers in Yakutat.

> *All over,*
> he says.
> *They're on their way north*
> *to nest in the tundra.*

It's hard to imagine
flying all that way
just to build a nest.

> *How about a duet?* Dad asks,
> holding up Grandma Jo's violin.

So I sing a song from our favorite movie
about a girl
and her family of voyagers.

When I get to the chorus, Dad is
plucking strings
drumming fingers
sounding like a whole orchestra
behind my melody.

But there's a delay in the video call,
and it's impossible to be exactly in sync.
Sometimes the screen freezes
and I just have to keep singing,
hoping we're staying on the same beat.

9
DREW

Most days, our runs sort of . . . run together. But one morning, Mia's already waiting when I come down the stairs. She's grinning like a Minion and hiding something in her hands.

"What have you got there?" Dad asks as he stretches his calves.

When Mia opens her hands, I'm just confused. Did she take my wooden bird out of the shop window? Why?

But Dad just laughs. "Plot twist! I never thought I'd see this thing again." Dad takes the bird, then holds it out to show me. Now that I look closer, her bird is a little different than mine, and he carved her name in the bottom. "Sandpipers migrate, you know," he says, turning the bird over in his hand. "All the way up the coast. But they always find their way back."

Finally, it clicks in my brain what this little bird means, and my mind is officially blown.

"Wait, the other Birth Day baby was *you*?" I ask. "Did they tell you I wouldn't stop screaming until they put me next to you? Like a smoke alarm. Want me to demonstrate?"

Mia laughs, but she holds her hand out to stop me. "No thanks," she says. "Now where should I put this while we run? I don't really want to carry it the whole way. Maybe in the lemon tree?"

"No, no, no," I insist. "I've got a better spot." I lead her into the shop and show her where my bird sits on the windowsill. She settles hers in next to it, and we both just stand there a minute, staring at them. "You can come back in and get it before you go home," I say. But something inside me wishes they could stay together like this, even if I know this isn't really where her bird belongs.

Five sweaty miles later, we're back in the shop, and Mia's reaching for the bird and getting ready to go when Dad interrupts us.

"Hey, could you guys help me with something for a second? I'm still catching up after my trip to the city."

I sigh and turn to Mia to apologize, but she's already headed toward him like she can't wait for whatever this is.

On the back worktable, Dad has spread out slabs of walnut. (I know it's walnut because the work order on his clipboard says so, not because I can actually tell the difference.)

"Oh, wow," Mia says. "Are you making somebody's front door?"

I'm about to tell her Dad always lays the pieces out flat like this and it's probably going to be a cabinet or something, but luckily, I keep my mouth shut.

"Good eye, Mia," Dad says. "Did you just fit the pieces together in your mind?"

"I guess," she says. "And it looks thicker than anything you'd use for cabinets. Is it walnut?"

"Yup," I say, stepping between them and surprising myself when I notice a little ping of jealousy. "Solid walnut. Two and a half inches thick," I add, glad that at least one other detail from the clipboard jumped out at me.

"I usually label the pieces, but it must have slipped my mind, so I'm hoping you can help me. You'll need to put them together like a puzzle. Rails go across, stiles go up and down, panels go in between, and there are a couple of mullions between those. And this puzzle can actually be put together a couple of different ways, so think about what fits best, but also how it looks right." Dad claps his hands and grins like he's giving us a gift or something. "What do you think? Want to take a crack at it?"

That all sounds like a little much to me. Mia, on the other hand, is already circling the table, running her fingers over the pieces, so what can I do but jump in? We both help, flipping and moving parts, trying the panels one way, then the other. But it's pretty clear Mia is the MVP of our team.

When we're finished, Dad comes back over to check our work. "Wow, you did it. I mean, you really did it." He looks at Mia. "I can tell you've got a mind for building things. I probably would have gotten it eventually, but I actually think the grains look better the way you've lined them up."

Mia smiles so big I'm afraid her cheeks will crack. "Who's it for?" she asks, and I'm curious about the answer too. Now that I see it like this, I can also imagine how it will look, and I realize my dad can make a heck of a door out of a stack of walnut boards.

"It's a commission for some guy in the city," Dad says. "I made him pay for the whole thing up front since a buddy of mine says he has a reputation for trying to dodge payments. Sometimes all it takes is one weasel like that to throw off your whole operation."

Mia has picked up the clipboard. She's staring down at it like she's just seen the Blue Lady, so I give her a little nudge with my elbow.

"Right, yeah, that makes sense," she says, dropping the clipboard and grabbing her bird from the windowsill. "I better go home now, but thanks again for letting us help. Maybe we can do it again sometime."

"I'd love that," Dad says. Then he looks over at me and laughs. "Don't worry, Drew. You don't have to participate. I know I promised you wouldn't have to help out until next summer."

"Nah, it's okay," I say, and I'm kind of surprised how much I mean it.

"Want to walk me out?" Mia asks. The shop door is like twenty feet away and Mia definitely knows how to get there, but something in her voice tells me I'd better come along.

"Sure," I say, nice and casual.

Once we're outside, Mia grabs my arm and drops her voice to a whisper.

"I think I might know him. Or, at least, know of him."

"Him who?" I ask, more confused than ever.

"The guy your dad is building the door for. And I might know how to help my family now."

10
MIA

LUCAS MARTIN

Back at home, I hurry to the box of important papers
to make sure the name on Pete's clipboard
matches the name on the file
with the red sticker.

It does.
The folder holds an invoice Dad's company sent
for a man named Lucas Martin to pay,
and the number on it looks huge to me.

But now there's another paper in the file
with the words *OFFER TO PURCHASE*
across the top in dark, dangerous ink.

Lucas Martin has made an offer
to buy our house.

The paper shakes in my hands,
but I take a deep breath,
put the folder back exactly where I found it.
Then I search his name
on my phone.

The second I see the smug smile
and perfectly clipped hair,
I remember.

Last spring, I visited Dad
at a renovation his crew was framing
in a historic neighborhood.

All the signs said Lucas Martin Construction,
but the only thing Lucas Martin did when I was there
was give a tour
to a camera crew.

He's auditioning for the Home Channel, Dad whispered
as Martin checked his hair in the camera lens.
He's pretending he knows everything that's going on here,
but today's the first day I've even seen him on-site.
He's still making excuses for why
he hasn't given us our first payment.
My crew will never work for him again.

Now I look at Martin's face on the screen and wonder:
Does the red sticker mean he *still* hasn't paid?
And if he did, would it be enough to keep our house?

THE PLAN: PART 1

I imagine myself
back in the woodshop;
the feeling
of working and thinking
and solving the puzzle of Pete's door.

Maybe I am a person who can make things right.
A person who sings my melody,
even when I can't hear my dad's harmony.

I search Lucas Martin's name again,
call the number on the screen,
leave a message when it goes straight to voice mail.

Hello, Mr. Martin.
My name is Mia Fisher
and I want to talk to you
about the house on McCallister.

I write the same words in an email.

I find pictures of him online:
>   Smug
>>   on his company website
>>   in a fancy suit
>>   and in staged photos of construction sites.
>   Standing
>>   with a surfboard,
>>   a fishing rod,
>>   two huge guys in San Francisco Giants uniforms.
>   Smiling a real smile
>>   in photos
>>   at the same finish lines
>>   for the last four years.

He's a runner.
I hate that we have that in common.
I hate that we have *anything* in common.

HIDING SOMETHING

After a few days,
there's no response from Martin,
but there's still plenty to keep me busy.

One day, the twins wake up with fevers
and Gram sends me to the pharmacy after lunch
to pick up more grape-flavored Tylenol—
the only kind they will take.

While I'm there, I see Pete
waiting patiently as a woman rings up
a whole pile of prescriptions.

Hi, Pete! I say.

> He startles,
> blocks the pile with his body
> like maybe he doesn't want me to see.
>
> *Drew's at the soda fountain getting ice cream,*
> he says. *You should go up there and say hi.*

So I go find Drew and slide onto the stool next to him.
He doesn't even notice I'm there until
I grab the spoon from his shake.

> Drew tugs it away,
> tries to laugh.
> He grabs a paper cup,
> scoops half his ice cream into it.
> *Have more if you want,*
> he says, sneaking a glance back at his dad.
> *I'm not as hungry as I thought I'd be.*

Maybe whatever Pete is hiding
is not as hidden as he thinks.

THE PLAN: PART 2

As I eat my ice cream,
I look at the world outside
through the patchwork of colorful flyers
hanging on the windows
until my gaze catches a green one
so far in the corner
I should have missed it.

The logo at the top looks like it matches the one
on Lucas Martin's T-shirt in those finish-line pictures
year after year.
I pull out my phone
to make sure.

It does.
And under the logo are the words
Half Moon Bay Half Marathon.

I still hate that we have anything in common,
but maybe there's a way to use it
to make things right.
To build myself
a backup plan.

I can keep calling, keep emailing.
That way, even if Lucas Martin never responds,
when I finally see him—
when I confront him face-to-face—
he will know
my name.

I pull the flyer from the window.
Press it into Drew's hand.

We should run this.

        He holds it up to get a better look.
        You're joking, right?

I have to, I say.
*And I don't think I can do it
alone.*

11
DREW

I stare at Mia, then at the flyer she just handed me.

Mia.

Flyer.

Mia.

Flyer.

She can't be serious.

"Do you even know how long a half marathon is?" I ask.

"No," she admits. "How long is it?"

"I have no idea! That's why *no* is the only appropriate answer."

Mia searches the flyer. "It's 13.1 miles. We can totally run that far! I bet we ran six miles this morning. That's almost halfway."

"I'll cheer for you at the finish line."

"Please," she begs. It freaks me out how serious she looks.

"Why are you suddenly all in on this thing you didn't even know about five minutes ago?"

Mia takes a deep, careful breath. She sits back down on the stool next to me. "Because there's a guy who runs it every year and I have to talk to him. The walnut-front-door guy. The guy who might be able to help us keep our house."

I spin on my stool, back and forth like a windshield wiper, because right now it's impossible to sit still. "Okay, so why do we have to run it? Why can't we just watch for him at the finish line?"

"Because," she says. Then she leans forward and says the next part low, like a secret. "Because I'll have thirteen miles to find him, when everybody is spread out along the trail instead of all in a crowd. Because it links us together and shows him we have something in common. Because he can't run away from me if he's already running and I'm running too." Mia grabs my shoulder to stop me from spinning. "Because it feels like we've been training for this all summer and just didn't know it until now."

"So I guess this is an important talk we're having right now."

"Yes," Mia says. "Yes."

I stare at her. "I . . . still have questions."

"Questions about what?" Dad asks. I have questions for him too, like why it took him so long to get his prescriptions and what exactly is in the bags. But I'm not sure I really want to know.

"Check it out, Pete." Mia hands Dad the flyer. "Don't you think we should run this together? All of us?"

Dad's eyes light up, which means I'm doomed.

"Absolutely! Amarante is always telling me I should run this."

Amarante is the nicest guy in the shop, but suddenly he's on my bad list.

Dad pulls up the calendar on his phone. "We have six weeks. That's plenty of time, considering how far we're running already. Let's do this."

Mia and Dad are smiling at each other like fools, but the whole thing feels off-balance.

Like maybe we've gotten so good at running this summer that we're all just running away from what scares us—like the bottles in that prescription bag.

Is it a good idea to make a promise to run more than ever?

Back at home, Dad starts turning table legs and I set up at my drawing desk. How is the summer almost halfway over and I've only filled a few pages of my sketchbook?

I pull up the photo I took today of the old-fashioned soda fountain and try to capture the feeling of the place with my pencil. The checkered tiles on the floor are pretty easy, but the chrome of the spinning stools takes a little more work. When I'm done, it all looks like some scene from the 1950s. Like it's trying to pull me to the past. I remember what Dad said to me the morning of our first run.

With a name like Drew, of course you were going to draw.

Even though "Draw" would be a ridiculous name, there's something sad about being named Drew. Past tense. Like what you are is already done. Already behind you.

But is present tense really better? It lasts forever, or only a second. Just depends on how you look at it.

Example: School is only a few weeks away, and I know that will come way before I'm ready. Then the race, and then my birthday. I'll be a teenager, which isn't totally a kid anymore. The school year will go by in a blur and then it'll be summer again but I'll be working in the shop, and where did all that time go? You can try to catch it in time capsules or art or museums or by building old-fashioned soda fountains, but that doesn't slow any of it down one bit.

I take a deep breath and turn to a new page, because what else can you do?

12
MIA

LOST AND FOUND

We start training for the race,
and there is purpose in my stride
to match the purpose in my plan.

Each day, after we run,
I peek through the woodshop window
and remember how it looked
when my little bird sat beside Drew's
and think of the day we helped Pete
with the walnut door.

Even though I only worked there once,
I miss the shop,
maybe because I miss working
on the house
with my hands
with my dad.

So one morning,
I bring the old violin back
and ask Drew a question:

*Do you think I could work on this
in your dad's shop?*

WHAT IT TAKES

After our run,
Drew shows me the spare parts
and teaches me the basics about stringed instruments
he knows from his guitar.

Since we both have babysitting duty in the afternoons,
we make a plan for our mornings:
Drew will draw
while I work on fixing up the violin.

Pete's around too, which sometimes helps
when Drew and YouTube can't.

> *This is a big project,*
> he says as he hands me fine sandpaper
> and teaches me how to work with the grain
> to make things smooth again.
> *It's a lot more delicate than anything I'm doing.*
> *It takes the right kind of person*
> *to make an instrument sing*
> *when it's been sitting silent this long.*
> *But I can tell you've got what it takes.*

What do I have?
And what does it take?

Then the label
of Pete's sandpaper
catches my attention
and I smile:

Grit.

GRIT

I leave another message.
Hello, Mr. Martin.
My name is Mia Fisher
and I want to talk to you
about the house on McCallister.

Seven miles.
Afterward, Drew draws the sea,
and I realize what's making the rattling sound
when a small piece of wood
falls out of the violin.

Another email.
Hello, Mr. Martin.
My name is Mia Fisher
and I want to talk to you
about the house on McCallister.

Five miles.
The small piece of wood
turns out to be a soundpost,
and it is surprisingly easy to put back in place
with the right tool
(and a little help from Pete).
Drew draws our running shoes.
Neither of us wanted to run this morning
but we did it anyway
and our shoes carried us every step.

Another phone call.
Hello, Mr. Martin.
My name is Mia Fisher
and I want to talk to you
about the house on McCallister.

Eight miles.
We don't work together in the shop
because I have to babysit this morning,
but I watch videos
about how to fix the bridge
that holds up the strings.

I fill out the contact form on the website.
Again.
Hello, Mr. Martin.
My name is Mia Fisher
and I want to talk to you
about the house on McCallister.

Five miles.
I fix the bridge
while Drew draws
the Golden Gate Bridge
from a postcard we find in the drawer.

Hello, Mr. Martin.
My name is Mia Fisher
and I want to talk to you
about the house on McCallister.

Nine miles.
I sand out more scratches.
Drew draws our favorite foods
because we talked about food
for nine whole miles.
(He says hamburgers
are harder to draw
than birthday cake.)

Hello, Mr. Martin.

Four miles.
I take the bridge back off
to put the varnish on
while Drew draws cartoons
of Owen and Oliver
and Luna.

My name is Mia Fisher

Nine miles.
I have to babysit early again,
but the varnish needs another day to dry anyway.

and I want to talk to you

Four miles.
The bridge goes up again
with the strings to press it down
but also
to keep it standing up.
This time,
Drew stops drawing
to help.

about the house on McCallister.

Ten miles.
Since Drew helped me yesterday,
I tell him I will draw with him today,
and he says we should draw each other.
Drew's picture looks just like me,
and mine looks like
a nightmare,
and we laugh
so hard our sides hurt,
and then everything else
from running ten miles
hurts a little less.

Hello, Mr. Martin.
My name is Mia Fisher
and I want to talk to you
about the house on McCallister.

HERE, THERE, NOWHERE

Grandma Jo was getting better
until she wasn't.

Until she died,
peacefully, in her sleep,
which is supposed to make me feel better
but doesn't at all,
especially when I see the letter she sent me
just last week
and remember the small stack of letters
in a storage locker in Sacramento
that I never even answered.

The funeral is short
and right to the point,
just like she wanted it,
just like Grandma Jo herself.

We gather on the couch:
>me then Owen then Mom then Oliver then Gram
>(so the boys can't pester each other)

and watch on the laptop
as Dad and Aunt Penny tell stories
about how Grandma Jo came to Yakutat
on a research trip in college
and was so in love with the place
and the people
that she never left.
About how she could cook just about anything
and fix anything too.

When it's time to scatter the ashes,
Owen and Oliver squirm until
they're allowed to run away,
and eventually Mom and Gram
go to look for them.

But I stay,
wishing I was there
with the mountains standing guard behind me
and the clear blue water in front of me
and Dad steady beside me.

Instead, I am here,
staring at the screen of Mom's laptop
until Dad comes and blows me a kiss
and turns the camera off.

For a second, the screen freezes,
and it's only once he's no longer moving
that I notice
how red Dad's eyes are.
How heavy the empty urn looks
in his hand.

Then, the screen goes black,
and for a moment,
it feels like I am nowhere at all.

SAID/SHOULD HAVE SAID

Things I said before Dad left:
Don't go.
Grandma Jo will be fine.
We need you here.
We have to finish the house.
Maybe you could just go for a day or two?

Things I should have said:
I'm sad, but I understand.
Grandma Jo hasn't seen you in years,
so I can share you for one summer.
You should go,
just in case she . . .
just in case.

What I want now
is to rewind
and repair.

Because how can I possibly be the person
who fixes things for other people
when all I do is think about myself?

SHARED LOCATION

The next morning,
when my alarm goes off at 5:30,
I silence it and close my eyes
and sleep until Gram comes to tell me
it's time for lunch.

When I check my phone
to see if it's really lunchtime,
I have a bunch of texts from Drew.

But I don't want to talk to anybody,
and the twins are asking to borrow my phone
to play *TitanIAm*.
I don't know what I'd say anyway.

So I ignore the texts
and hand off my phone
and try to sleep some more.

By the time I get my phone back after dinner,
there are more texts
(all from Drew)
because
of course
not reading them
doesn't make them go away.

6:03 a.m.: *Where are you*

6:05 a.m.: *We are waiting 5 more min then we are leaving*

7:12 a.m.: *I ran 7 miles at a record pace and didn't even break a sweat and no you don't need to verify any of that with my dad k thanks*

10:24 a.m.: *Where are you??*

10:25 a.m.: *Nobody is working on your violin so I am drawing your violin so it won't be lonely*

10:27 a.m.: *Now I am painting your violin*

10:27 a.m.: *Wait no I'm not painting your actual violin HA! sorry if that freaked you out*

10:28 a.m.: *I am painting a picture of your violin*

2:32 p.m.: *I am finished with the painting and it is a freaking masterpiece and probably worth millions*

2:33 p.m.: *And no you don't need to verify that with actual art critics k thanks*

2:42 p.m.: *WHERE ARE YOU??*

4:47 p.m.: *WHERE ARE YOU??*

6:16 p.m.: *WHERE ARE YOU??*

6:17 p.m.: *WHERE ARE YOU??*

6:18 p.m.: *WHERE ARE YOU??*

I know I should text Drew back,
but I can't think of anything to say
and the twins want my phone back
to play more *TitanIAm* anyway.

So I clear my dishes and climb back in bed.
I am trying to decide if I want Owen and Oliver
to climb in beside me
when Gram's doorbell rings.

I hear Drew's voice
and feel so guilty and embarrassed
for not answering him
that I pretend to be asleep.

After he leaves,
Mom comes in quietly
and sets something on my desk.
As soon as she closes my door,
I sneak over to look.

It's Drew's painting of my violin,
thick paint on a smooth scrap of wood,
and it's so beautiful
and so thoughtful
that I turn his masterpiece around
because I don't deserve it.

How does he know where I live? I wonder aloud
as Owen and Oliver burst through the door.

We shared your location, says Owen.

He kept texting
when we were trying to play TitanIAm
on your phone, says Oliver.

Can we play TitanIAm *on your phone now?* asks Owen.

Okay, I say, *but only for a few minutes.*
And you have to play it in here.

Okay, they say at the same time,
and we all climb into my bed together
and things do feel
just a little more
okay.

ALL IN

The next morning,
on our run,
I thank Drew for the painting.
Tell him about the funeral
and all the letters from Grandma Jo
I never answered.

I start it as a confession
of how selfish I've been,
but Drew disagrees.

> *You're not selfish.*
> *You've spent this whole summer*
> *trying to track down that Martin guy*
> *and save your family's house.*
> *I mean, at this point,*
> *you're trying so hard to help*
> *you're borderline stalking somebody.*

Speaking of which,
I think it's a good idea to move into phase two.
We focus on the race,
let him think you've given up,
and then BAM.
There you are, in person,
right when he's exhausted
and his guard's down.

And the violin.
The violin!
You don't even play.
You've been fixing it for your dad all along.
How could that be selfish?

You need to give yourself a break, Mia.
Or not a break, I guess,
since what you're doing matters
and yesterday was super boring without you.
But give yourself some credit at least.

We've been running for miles
and still have miles ahead of us,
but in that moment,
with Drew by my side
and his words in my head,
I feel like I could run forever.
Like I can go all in.
On the fight to keep our house.
On finishing the violin for Dad.
And for Grandma Jo.

*Are you this good
at solving everybody's problems?* I ask.

I wish, says Drew.
Then, softer,
I wish.

13
DREW

The weeks fly by, just like I knew they would. Mia and I keep running, alternating shorter runs with longer and longer ones—although part of me still can't believe that four miles is "short." My new shoes definitely don't smell like the Nike factory anymore, but somehow they fit even better, like they've learned every curve and callus of my feet.

Dad still runs with us, even if he turns around early sometimes. But suddenly he really likes to swim laps at the high school pool too. Since I'm still limited to one hour of *TitanIAm* and Mia has to help with her brothers during the day, guess who gets dragged along? At least it's only on my four-mile days. One time, after we get out of the pool, Dad catches me looking at the scar on his knee from his fall, clear back on the first day Mia ran with us.

"Pretty impressive, huh?" He closes his eyes before he gets up from the locker room bench. He's worn out. Between the running and the swimming, I'm worn out too, but it's different. Present-tense tired that will soon be left in the past. With Dad, it feels like his worn out stretches all the way into the future too.

That night, Dad falls asleep before dinner. Mom tells me not to wake him up. "He'll eat when he's hungry," she says. "You know what would be nice? You could write him a note and sneak it into his suitcase."

"Where's he going?" I ask.

"To the city for a couple of days. Can you get the travel pillow from the hall closet?"

"The city again? Why?"

She hesitates. "He'll tell you about it. You can ask him when he wakes up."

I'm not really a note writer, and he'd probably like a drawing better anyway, so I work on my soda fountain sketch until it looks decent, add a quick *Thanks for the ice cream* on the bottom, and take it to his room with the travel pillow. It's so quiet in there that I'm sure he'll wake up when I unzip the front pocket of the suitcase, but his breathing stays smooth and steady.

The sketch slides in nicely—until it doesn't. I thought the front pocket was empty, but there's something jammed at the bottom. Something flat and plastic. Whatever it is, I don't want it messing up the sketch, so I pull it out.

Even in the little beam of light from the open doorway, I can tell what it is.

A hospital bracelet.

I have one too, from the time I got my tonsils out. But

there's no reason Dad should have one now. No reason I can think of that doesn't take my brain straight to panic mode.

There are letters and a date printed on it, and I try to remember if it matches the date my parents went to the "work conference" in the city.

"Dad," I say, not even quietly.

He doesn't move.

"Dad." A little louder. Suddenly, Mom's standing in the doorway.

"Don't wake him up, Drew. He's really tired."

I hold up the hospital bracelet. "Are you sure he's just 'tired'?"

She can't tell what it is until she kneels beside me. When she realizes, she takes in a sharp breath.

"He'll tell you when he wakes up," she says. "He doesn't want you to worry."

I stand up. "Too late. Tell me yourself."

She looks away. "It's not my story to tell. I promised. He'll be up soon, though. He'll need his medicine."

"Then I'll wait."

I sit on the chair in the corner. The one my grandfather built.

Mom nods. She leaves, I wait.

Finally, Dad rolls over and rubs his eyes.

"Hey, Drew," he says. "Is it already time to run?"

He thinks it's tomorrow, but it's still today, and apparently today's the day everything changes. I can feel it. He sits up—is he struggling because he's sick, or because he's tired?—and I set the bracelet on his nightstand.

"Mom said it was your story to tell. So tell me." I swallow hard, but the knot stays in my throat. "Please."

"Okay," he says. He pushes back the covers and sits up slowly. Then he says it again, like he's really awake. "Okay." He presses his lips together while he figures out what to say. Finally, he looks up, and it's hard to tell in the dark, but it almost looks like there are tears in his eyes.

"We both know Willie Mays is the best ball player of all time, but have you ever heard of Lou Gehrig?"

I grab the bracelet back and hold it in front of his face. "We're not talking about baseball. You're telling me about this."

He takes the bracelet from me. Real gentle. "I'm trying. This is the only way I know to get it out. Lou Gehrig. You heard of him?"

I give in. "Yeah, I've heard of him. He played for the Yankees. He was on that ESPN special we watched. Greatest sports speeches of all time."

He nods. "Today. . ." There's a sound like a sob, but he clears his throat and tries again. "Today I feel like the luckiest man alive."

Then I remember. Lou Gehrig gave that speech because he was retiring.

He gave that speech because he was dying.

I can't look at Dad, so I stare at the bracelet instead.

"Do you have what he had?" In my gut, I already know the answer. But I need to hear him say it.

"I have what he had. Amyotrophic lateral sclerosis. ALS." He takes a big breath. "Lou Gehrig's disease. I'm sorry I didn't tell you sooner. I wanted us to have one last, best summer before everything changed."

One last, best summer before everything changed. That's exactly what I wanted too, ever since I went looking for that time capsule. Only Dad's best summer was all about being with me, and I've been low-key complaining about it the whole time.

I think I might be sick.

My mind races and reaches for an escape hatch. "But that Lou Gehrig video was black and white. He lived a long time ago. They probably figured out a cure by now, right?"

He lays a hand on my shoulder and looks me straight in the eye. "Not yet, but they're working on it. There are better treatments now than there were then. And you know I'm doing everything I can to take care of myself."

"So, what happens? Your body just shuts down?"

He looks away. "Not all at once, and not anytime soon. I might trip a little more, drop things. Eventually it'll be more than that, but most of the time it happens really slowly."

"Does it ever reverse?"

He shakes his head.

"So you trip and drop stuff, and then it gets worse. Like what? Then after a while you can't walk? You can't eat?" As I gulp in air, I realize something even worse.

"After a while you can't breathe?"

He doesn't answer. He doesn't need to.

It all makes sense now: the running, the swimming, the medicine, the mysterious trips and talk about miraculous bodies.

"Thanks for telling me," I say, even though I'm not sure I mean it.

He leans back on his pillows. "It feels better now that it's not a secret. Ask me anything, anytime." Maybe it's the fading light or maybe it's the things he just told me, but time is moving so fast and he looks so old. So tired.

"I have to go," I say. I want to hug him, but I can't. Because what will happen if I put my arms around him and that feels different too?

Down the hall, Mom is reading Luna a bedtime story. There's a sad note in her voice. Has it been there all summer? When would they have told me if I hadn't found that bracelet?

I pause in Luna's doorway. Mom looks up, tears in her eyes. "Did he . . ."

"Yeah."

"Are you going down to the beach?"

"Yeah."

"Be back in an hour, okay?"

"Okay."

We look at each other for a second, and I hope hope hope she'll say something because my words are all gone now. I want her to tell me to crawl under the covers with them and read *All the World* together and feel like this life is full of hope and peace and love and trust.

But she doesn't. So maybe they've been lying about that too.

I don't know if I ever ran all the way from my house to the ocean before this summer, but I don't even realize I've done it until I'm almost there. I'm not even breathing hard. I'm stronger and faster than I've ever been, and suddenly I hate that about myself. How is that fair at all?

Part of me just wants to keep running right into the water, then swim a straight line as far as my muscles can go. And then what?

Then what?

What makes your body decide that it's going to stop doing the things it's been doing all your life? That one more step or stroke is just too many? That maybe it's time to just shut it all down?

When I look out into the ocean, it's too black, too big. Who was I kidding? The Pacific is the biggest ocean in the whole world, and tonight I don't even dare step into it. So instead, I throw stones and shells and whatever else I can grab, one after another. I start throwing faster and farther, always reaching for the next thing I can chuck out into the cold, dark water.

Most of the time, you can't even see a splash when you throw something into the ocean. Not when the sun is down and the waves are coming in—and the waves are always, always coming in. So I'm not sure how many extra splashes there have been when I realize somebody is throwing next to me. At first I think maybe it's Mia, but then I turn to look and it's not.

It's Isaac.

I haven't seen him in three months. There should be so much to say. Plus, it's *Isaac*, who always has plenty to talk about.

But he just nods.

Picks up another stone.

Throws again.

So I do too.

"I'll be here all weekend. You want to hang out tomorrow?" he asks after a while.

Do I? I don't know how I'm supposed to think past the next breath. The next stone.

"Maybe."

"Okay," he says.

"Okay," I say, and then I can't breathe for a second. "Not okay. My dad's not okay." Then it all comes flooding out: the suitcase, the bracelet, the confession. The disease.

When I'm done, there's nothing to say and way too much. So we just stay there like that, launching stones, until I know it's been so long Mom might be getting worried. She doesn't need another thing to worry about, so I grab one last handful of stones and give them to Isaac.

He doesn't even ask what to do or why. He just knows. When I get to the path, I turn around, and sure enough, he's chucking those stones into the ocean, one by one. For me.

14
MIA

TICKETS

I'm helping clear the dinner dishes
when Mom takes Oliver's plate from my hand.

I'll finish that up, she says.
Gram has a surprise for you.

Gram is waiting, smiling.
She hands me two tickets, says,
Our local theater company does quite a nice job,
if I can steal you away from your friend for a night.

I'm so tired from running
and from chasing my brothers all day
that I want to climb in bed right now,
especially since we're running ten tomorrow.

But then I slide my finger along
the gold strip at the tickets' edge.
Gram has gone into town to pick them up
instead of just printing them at home.
She has curled her hair
and is wearing pink lipstick.

> *It's one of my favorites,* she says,
> hope in her voice.

Our Town? I ask, still unsure.
Is it about Half Moon Bay?

> Gram smiles.
> *Yes and no.*
> *You'll see what I mean.*

So I thank Gram
and put on the blue dress
and we drive to a small theater
and let one of Gram's friends scan our tickets
and find our seats.

I almost wonder if we're in the right place
or here at the right time
since there's no curtain
and no scenery
and a man in a hat
with a pipe in his mouth
is carrying tables and chairs
onto the stage.

But when he's finished,
the lights go down,
and when it's dark,
he speaks,
and the play
begins.

OUR TOWN

In the middle of the first act,
I remember the question I asked Gram:

Is this play about Half Moon Bay?

and I realize she was right.

It's really about a town called Grover's Corners
and characters called Emily and George,
but kind of,
it's about Half Moon Bay
and me and Drew
and anywhere you might ever live
and anyone you might ever meet.

It's about family and friends
and community.

It's about life.
And it's about death.

When the lights come up
to start Act III,
I realize the chairs on the stage
are supposed to be headstones,
and the people in them
are supposed to be dead.

Act III is going to be about death
and the Stage Manager tried to warn us.

I look to Gram,
suddenly wanting to leave.

Because even though it's just chairs
and strangers
on an empty stage,
it's also
the bay where they scattered Grandma Jo's ashes
and I can almost see her
there among the dead,
staring back at me like all the others
without seeing me at all.

Gram reaches over,
squeezes my hand,
whispers:
Look. Listen.

So I do.
I listen to every word,
and I don't look away,
even when the tears
begin to pool in my eyes.

IMPORTANT ENOUGH: PART 1

Afterward, Gram and I are quiet
as we walk to the car.

I am thinking about Emily:
how she was one of the dead,
but she realized she could go back,
so she did.

The others told her
to choose an ordinary day.
That even the most ordinary day
would be important enough.

But she didn't listen.
She chose her twelfth birthday
and when she went back
it was too much for her
to see
really see
the people who loved her
and the little things that make a life.

It was too much for me too.

I am still twelve
and yet
I barely remember any of my last birthday
because I wasn't really looking
or listening.
I just took it all for granted.

I can't remember
what color Owen's eyes are
or what books Oliver likes best at bedtime.
I don't know whether Mom has ever seen *Our Town*
or whether Dad has ever played baseball
or how they met each other.

When Emily asked her most important question,
about whether anybody ever realizes
every minute of their life
right when they live it,
I answered with the Stage Manager
in the softest whisper
as the tears traced down my cheeks.
No.

You're deep in thought,
Gram says as we turn out of the parking lot.
Anything you want to talk about?

What day would you choose? I ask.
I know the whole point
was that they all matter,
but still, I want to know.

Gram thinks about it a moment,
then squeezes my hand and says,
I think today would be about as fine a day as any.

I squeeze her hand back.
Then I imagine Grandma Jo's hand in my other hand
and squeeze it too.

IMPORTANT ENOUGH: PART 2

When we get home,
Mom and the twins are already asleep,
and Gram yawns
as she hangs up her keys
on the hook in the kitchen.

But my heart is full and my mind is racing,
so instead of putting on pajamas,
I pull out my notebook.

All summer,
I have been writing
just to fill the pages,
even when I'm not sure
whether what happened
is important.

But now I know:
It is important enough.

So I stay up for hours,
writing the memory of this night,
wanting to remember all the details
before the tide of my own forgetting
washes them away too.

ACT III

I meant to write all night,
but I must have fallen asleep.
There's a gentle glow through my window,
and the clock on my nightstand tells me
it's time to get ready to run.

I can't wait to tell Drew and Pete
about the play.
It feels a little like
what Pete's been telling us all along
about our amazing bodies
and the incredible world we're part of.

Now, like him,
I want to make the most of this life—
every, every minute.

But when I get to Drew's,
something's different.
And not just because his friend Isaac shows up too.

Something has shifted
or maybe even broken,
and all I can think about
are Pete's feet stumbling
and his body hiding the prescriptions
at the pharmacy.

Even though I don't know exactly what's wrong,
I know enough.
Because even though they're trying to hide it,
when I look
and listen,
there's something
hushed
haunted
in everything Drew and Pete
and even Isaac
say
or don't say
or do
or don't do.

Almost like they already saw Act III
but they're trying to pretend they didn't.

For a second,
I want to tell them
        that we really do have the power
                to fix things,
                to choose,
                to change our circumstances.

But maybe that's not true
when it comes to the kind of problem that requires
bags of orange prescription bottles.

Before I can find
the right words,
we are running,
and it is all I can do
to keep up.

15
DREW

Once upon a time, Isaac and I had plans:

Spend every birthday together.

Spend every summer together.

Best friends for life.

And okay, he sort of abandoned me when he moved to the city, but maybe the last one isn't ruined yet. Because even though I haven't seen him all summer, he showed up right at the moment I needed him most. And maybe it didn't fix anything, but it helped a little.

So when I got home last night, I sent him a text.

Thanks for being there tonight.
Want to go running tomorrow morning?

Now here he is, standing under the lemon tree at 6:00 a.m.

"Dude," I say, slapping him on the back as soon as I get down the stairs. "You came."

Luckily, Isaac gets the message that we're not talking about the stuff we talked about on the beach last night.

"Of course I came. Remember how loud my grandpa snores? I was up anyway."

Dad finally comes down. "Isaac!" he says. "We've missed you." He rests a hand on my shoulder while he grabs a toe to stretch his quads. "We were going to run ten this morning. Is that too far? If you want to turn around early, I can turn around with you."

Isaac laughs. "Ten *miles*? Yeah, that might be a little much. I'll go as far as I can, but don't let me hold you back. You guys should totally run ten. We can meet back here after."

Mia has been watching us quietly, but then she walks right up to Isaac and sticks her hand out. "I'm Mia," she says. "And I'm betting you're Isaac."

It's just Mia, but Isaac lights up when she shakes his hand. "That's me," he says, giving her hand at least three more good shakes before he realizes he should probably let go.

We run together until Isaac and Dad turn around, and then Mia and I go on alone. When we finally get back, Dad's already in the shop and Isaac is passed out under the lemon tree. He really must not have gotten much sleep with his grandpa's snoring.

Mia and I flop on the grass next to him, and I immediately start pulling off my shoes. "Ahhh, sweet freedom for my poor feet," I say, tossing one stinky sock each at Isaac and Mia. "That was a long one. I think I lost about five pounds of sweat."

Mia throws the sock back in my face and flops down on her back next to Isaac.

Like, *right* next to Isaac.

"Cool grass is the greatest thing ever invented." She turns her head and smiles at Isaac, and he lights up again like a Christmas tree. "I can see how you fell asleep."

It's kind of cute, but I don't exactly want to watch, so I flop down on my back too, and the three of us are all staring up at the lemon branches crisscrossing between us and the sky.

"What should we do now?" I ask.

Mia sighs. "I would love to stay here forever, but I have to get home early today to watch my brothers. I can hang out tonight, though."

I roll over to my belly. "Yeah, tonight! Isaac, can you come to the beach tonight?"

"Sure," he says. "We're supposed to have a bunch of family time while we're here, but my parents promised me and Tam that we could do whatever we wanted for the first twenty-four hours."

It's not the same as a whole summer together, but I'll take it. Especially today. "Does that mean you can hang out here all day?" I ask. That would be the perfect distraction.

When he nods, I pump my fist. "We are going to play SO MUCH *TitanIAm*."

But we don't. After Mia leaves, we end up playing fetch with Scout and Luna for a while. (Luna insists.) Then Dad comes upstairs and asks us if we need anything at the grocery store, and Isaac has an idea.

"We could do a cookout. Do you usually eat when you go down to the beach?"

I slap my forehead. How did I never think of that? "No, but we totally should."

We get Dad's permission, then go with him to the store to pick up everything we'll need. By the time we get back, it's lunchtime, so Isaac makes his world-famous quesadillas, and then we ride our bikes to the cypress grove to look for the time capsule and play catch.

But even when we're standing there with our shovels (and our baseball gloves), neither of us has any idea where we buried the time capsule. How did we lose it so completely? Were we both so sure the other one would hold the memory that we didn't bother to remember ourselves?

Luckily, catch is harder to mess up. We get a nice rhythm going, and for the first time, the slap of the ball against the leather of Isaac's glove is just as loud as it is against mine. I'm throwing harder this year. I'm about to say something about that fact (in a trash-talk sort of way) when Isaac surprises me with a question.

"Do you want to talk about it?" he asks.

I frown. "And by it, you mean . . . the *it* from the beach?" This seems suspicious. "Should I?"

Isaac shrugs. "Mom and Dad made me start seeing a therapist when my grades tanked at the beginning of last year and I didn't want to talk about why. But then it turned out I kind of . . . did."

"I already talked about it, remember? Last night with the rock throwing?"

"You're right," he says.

Then it occurs to me that, even after all the hours we've spent on the phone while we play *TitanIAm*, I wouldn't say I know what's going on in Isaac's actual life.

"Your grades tanked?" I ask.

As we throw the ball back and forth in the swaying shadows of the cypress trees, he tells me. How his parents are fighting and his sister's gone all the time and playing *TitanIAm* is the best part of his life by about a million percent. How he took a cooking class in school last year and now he cooks all the time. (Which makes the shopping list he made for our cookout make a lot more sense.)

Even after Isaac gets quiet again, it takes a few more throws before I'm ready. "I stayed up late reading about ALS," I say, and then everything I can remember about Dad's disease spills out of me. By the time I'm done, I'm exhausted from the ten miles and the catch and everything else that's happened.

"It's not fair," Isaac says. "Your dad is one of the best guys I've ever met."

I take off my glove and slump against a tree trunk.

"Yeah, good point. Whoever is in charge of making life fair is doing a pretty crappy job."

Isaac leans against a tree right across from mine, and for the second time that day, we just sit there quietly, watching the play of light through leaves.

"You know what's missing in *TitanIAm*?" I say.

"Bathrooms?" Isaac says. And yeah, he has a point.

"Besides bathrooms. Oracles. Guides. Wise elders you can ask for help. I like the games where they have that. But in *TitanIAm*, they just drop you in the middle of some new world and expect you to figure it out for yourself." I sigh. "I feel like that just happened to me in real life. I sure could use a wise elder in real life right about now."

Isaac waggles his eyebrows. "Lucky for you, I'm four months older."

I roll my eyes. "Yeah. You're not exactly what I had in mind. It's okay, though. Let's just go home."

There's a two-count rhythm anytime you ride a bike, just like running, and today it's chanting at me: *not fair, not fair, not fair.* Because my dad really is one of the best guys ever, and he's dying. His body is shutting down. And there's nothing any of us can do about it.

Meanwhile, I'm totally fine, even though I can be a terrible person sometimes.

I've been lying to my parents about how much time I've spent gaming this summer.

And sometimes I ignore Luna.

Sometimes I ignore her *while* I'm breaking the screen-time rule.

Also, I saw the answers to a math test last year. I wasn't trying to, but I saw them, and I remembered some of them and put them on my test, and I didn't tell anybody.

And I can't even remember the last time I flossed.

I am the worst.

"Why do people like me get to live and the really good people have to die?"

Isaac's ahead of me, but he turns back, because apparently I asked the last question out loud. "What?" he asks, his head swiveling between me and the road ahead.

"Nothing," I shout. "It doesn't matter."

Even though it definitely does.

We're gliding downhill now, so I spin my pedals backward, wishing I could make time go backward too.

I picture Dad healthy and Isaac's family living here again. I see the whole world like a movie in reverse—sidewalk cracks uncracking, dead trees coming back to life, friendships back to good, for good. And even though it sounds dumber than rocks, I can almost picture the superhero from the comic Isaac and I made when we were kids, except he looks like me. If only I had actual superpowers to fix anything at all.

Later, Isaac and I load up a cooler with buns, ketchup, mustard, and hot dogs. We grab the chips and the guacamole Isaac made with a little lemon juice from one of the lemons on our tree, and at the last minute, I remember my guitar too.

At the beach, I build a fire while Isaac and Mia set up the food as the sun sinks toward the water. We all put Isaac's relish on our hot dogs and agree it's a lot better than the stuff you buy at the store, mostly because Isaac's is actually good.

I try to breathe deep and take it all in: same Isaac, same beach, same beat-up red cooler. But it still feels like the whole world has shifted this summer. Not that I expected everything to stay exactly the same. When you jump, you expect the earth to rotate a millionth of an inch. But this time, it's like the whole thing moved a mile while I was in the air, and a lot of it broke too.

We eat and we talk, though, and for a while things seem at least a little better. We tell Isaac about our birthday connection and then we all try to remember our favorite birthdays. Mine was the day I got Scout, but second place goes to the year I got my first basketball hoop—a little plastic one that I loved to bank shots on because it made the whole thing shake. For Isaac, it was turning ten and finally being old enough to surf. Mia's was the day her dad showed her where their house was going to be, but even though it's her favorite, she's kind of sad when she tells it. We're about to start another round when Isaac's phone buzzes.

"Sorry," he says. "I have to go, and I'm probably stuck with my family for the rest of this trip."

"Say hi to them for me," I say. "And tell them thanks for letting me hang out with you for the first twenty-four hours."

"Yeah, for sure," he says. "Good to meet you, Mia."

"Good to meet you too," she says. "Are you coming back some time?" She asks it pretty casual, but the electricity is back, for both of them.

"Not sure," he says. "Maybe for Drew's birthday?"

"And mine," Mia says.

But that's not what I'm focused on. "September? Are you serious? That's after school starts. It's only technically summer by then."

Isaac turns to me, and it's like I can see all the Isaacs I've known: the preschooler on a Halloween-candy high, the first baseman to my shortstop, the person who listened to me and let me talk about the hard stuff today.

"If you need me sooner," he says, "I'll find a way."

The thing about a best friend is, you believe them. And even if almost everything else in the world had changed, Isaac and I are still best friends.

After the last twenty-four hours, I know that for sure.

16
MIA

DUET: PART 2

Do you want to talk about it?

After Isaac leaves,
I'm lost in my own head,
wondering what it would have been like
if my Sacramento friends had been here too.

Thinking about the change in Drew
since this morning,
      now that he got to spend a day
      with the person he missed most.

I'm so lost I don't realize I'm lost at all
until Drew surprises me with his question.

DO I want to talk about it?
When I stop to think about it, I realize
I kind of do.

It feels good to talk to Drew
about Gram and *Our Town*
and Dad and Grandma Jo
and how I still haven't heard back from Lucas Martin
and how I'll be starting school here
and everything else.

When I'm all talked out,
Drew tunes his guitar,
I hum a little to warm up my voice.

Even though I know
there are always people around,
        surfers and tourists
        and joggers and families
now that Drew and I are finally here again,
the rest of the world
doesn't seem to matter much.

Still, people come closer when they hear us.
Stop to listen a little before moving on.
An old man drops a dollar in Drew's case.

We look at each other
and Drew mouths, *Buskers,*
and we almost burst out laughing,
which feels like exactly
what we both needed.

ADVICE

When we've played all the songs we know,
I sit back,
stretch my legs out.
Gather sand from the blanket
and drop it back onto the beach.

> Drew reaches over to help,
> but the grains of sand are so tiny
> and there are so many of them
> there's not much either of us can do.

What about you?
Do you want to talk about anything? I ask,
hoping he'll tell me
what's actually going on with his dad.

> Drew fingers a silent song on his guitar.
> *I think I'm done with talking.*
> *If I'm being honest,*
> *sometimes I kind of wish*
> *we were done with running too.*
> *Because no matter how fast or how far you run,*
> *sometimes the bad stuff catches up to you.*

I nod,
wishing I had the right words for this moment.
But maybe even when you don't know exactly what to say,
it's better to just say something.

I know I'm not Isaac,
but I'm here.
What would be the best thing
a friend could say to you right now?

Drew looks out at the water,
and I can almost see the moment
he realizes what he wants me to say.
That there are good things coming
as long as you have hope.
And the other thing I'd want you to say
you already said:
I'm here.

After that,
we roast marshmallows,
build sculptures in the sand,
and even though
the tide will wash it all away tomorrow,
I'm glad we built it tonight.

FIRST DAY: PART 1

In Sacramento,
school starts in September.
But here, it begins at the end of August,
even though the calendar says
there's nearly a month of summer left.

When morning comes,
I put on the blue dress,
a hint of the ocean
caught in the fabric.

Drew and I are running after school now,
so I pack shorts and shoes
in my backpack,
knowing that
when school starts in Sacramento,
my friends will be doing the same thing.

Then I wake the twins
(who snuck to my bed again)
and help button them into new, matching shirts.

They are excited for preschool
and want to trick their teacher,
which makes me smile.

Oliver wonders
if they could trick Dad now too,
which makes me sad.

How is it possible
Dad's been gone
almost three months?

I can already feel the rhythm
of starting a new routine.

But how can it be time
for new schedules and routines
when Dad never even saw the old ones?

Sometimes it feels like the wound
of his being gone
is healing,
then something so small rips it open
and I miss him all over again.

FIRST DAY: PART 2

Drew's waiting for me
in first period math.
I saved you a seat, he whispers,
even though everybody around us
is talking in totally normal voices.

Thanks, I whisper back.

When math is over, I'm the first one out the door,
tilting my face upward to drink in the sky.

There are no hallways in the school—
our classroom doors open right into
the fresh air I'm thirsty for.

Lunch is outside too,
and I sit with Drew's friends,
a mix of boys and girls who smile
but have too much to say to each other
after a long summer apart
to spend many words on me.

In Sacramento, Dad would try
to time his lunch break
so we could eat together once a month
because he knew I couldn't handle
the school lunch version
of Taco Tuesday.

Does he remember
how we'd drive to our favorite food truck
with the windows down
and the music turned up?

Drew and I are both slow eaters,
which means we're the last ones at the table,
which means he splits his cookie with me.

A boy with a smug smile stops at our table and leans over.

Finally found a girlfriend, Drew?

Drew stammers and sputters,
the kid smirks and walks away.

The trapped look on Drew's face makes me laugh.
Take it easy, I say.
I know I'm not your girlfriend.

Drew relaxes.
Are you looking for a boyfriend?
he asks, raising his eyebrows.
Because I can introduce you
to any guy at this school.

Now it's my turn to blush
as I break my cookie half
into bite-size pieces.
I haven't noticed anybody.
I mean, I have noticed people,
but not like that.
I mean . . .
(Most of my cookie is crumbs now.)
So are we running after school?

Drew says yes.

BETTER THAN

Drew runs beside me every mile that day
  and the next day,
  and every other school day
  for two weeks after that.
He sits beside me every day at lunch
and in the workshop
as he helps me put the finishing touches
on the violin.

A friend like that is
  better than a cookie
and probably
  better than a boyfriend too.

LAST WORKOUT

The night before the half marathon,
Drew shows up at my door,
holds out a cinch bag with a sporty logo on the side.

> *Your swag bag,* he says.
> *We're all checked in.*
> *Just pin the number to your shirt*
> *tomorrow morning.*
> *But right now, we have one last workout.*
> *My dad's orders.*

I thought today was a rest day,
but Gram shoos me out the door
where Pete is waiting in the car.

Back at Drew's house,
Scout's in the driveway,
wagging her tail.

I kneel, reach around to scratch her back
as she rests her chin on my shoulder.

I never wanted a dog
       but
I never knew one like Scout.

Come on, girl,
I say after a minute.
Let's get upstairs.

Inside, the air is warm
and heavy with garlic.
Luna comes over and holds out her chubby arms,
so of course I pick her up.

> *Hey, Mia,* says Drew's mom.
> *Have a seat.*
> *Ready for your last workout?*

I guess, I say,
still confused
as I look over the table,
already ringed with plates,
the center filled with
pots and platters.
Are we eating or running?

> Pete's still standing,
> gripping the back of the chair with one hand,
> reaching forward with the other.
> *Now, this really is a workout,*
> he says, lifting the lid off a giant pot of pasta.
> *It's a long, time-honored tradition*
> *to eat spaghetti before a big race.*

Don't make yourselves sick or anything.
(He's looking at Drew for that part.)
But eat as much as you can.
Tomorrow's road trip requires
a lot of fuel.
His arms shake a little
as he lowers himself into his seat.

So I follow Pete's instructions
and eat as much as I can,
savoring every single bite,
wondering for a second
if Lucas Martin is eating spaghetti tonight too,
and if I'll have the courage
to go through with my plan tomorrow.

When my pile has disappeared completely,
I scoop up the last bits of sauce with my garlic bread.

Luna's mouth is ringed with red
as she calls for *MORE PAGEPPI.*
Her mom puts a piece of garlic bread on her tray,
but that's not what Luna's after.
She windshield-wipers her hands so hard

                                          across the tray
the bread goes flying

                                          across the room
and cracks its own crust against the wall.

Wow, kid, Pete says. *That was really impressive.*
He stands up halfway,
leans over to grab it.

But then he falls
        forward,
                forward,
                        forward,
until his head cracks against the floor.

Drew and his mom rush to him,
kneel beside him,
roll him over.

There's no blood,
but his eyes are blank.
A low, moaning sound starts,
and I'm not even sure it's coming from him.

Then Luna's cry cuts through the night,
and I finally snap back into myself.
I lift her from the high chair,
hold her close,
whisper an almost-prayer in her ear.

        Please.
        Please.
        Please.

17
DREW

For the first time in my life, my fingers dial 9-1-1. I want to explain everything: what happened, where we live, how important it is for them to hurry. But the words stick in my mouth, so I pass the phone to Mom, hating that I can't even do this small thing to help.

Mia holds Luna in one arm and sticks a Post-it note in front of me with the other. She asks me a question, and I nod even though I didn't hear what she said.

Dad wakes up while we're waiting for the ambulance, but his words are too thick and heavy to understand. Mom doesn't get up from the floor until Dad is all the way on the stretcher and rolling toward the door. She's about to follow him out into the night, but then she turns back, like she forgot something.

Us. Mom forgot about us. I forgot about us too.

Mia didn't forget. "I found the list of emergency numbers in the kitchen," she tells Mom, "and I called your sister. I'll stay until she gets here. You can go."

Mom gives her a quick hug. "Thank you," she whispers.

Luna reaches for Mom, but Mia sways and bounces her until she laughs. "We'd better clean that face off, Luna-Lou. What jammies do you want tonight?"

When they go off down the hall, Mom turns to me. "I'm coming with you," I say. "Please." I'm too numb to feel much, but I know I need to be there.

Mom just nods, and we hurry out the door and toward the ambulance. "Follow us there," the EMT tells us as she latches the back.

So we tail the ambulance and run every red light it runs. At the hospital, they wave us over to the parking lot. By the time we find where they took Dad, they tell us we'll have to wait. Mom calls to check in with Aunt Shannon, and after that, we sit in scratchy chairs the color of dead grass. All we can do is exactly what they say—wait, wait, wait. When even your mom doesn't tell you *It's going to be okay*, you can be pretty sure it won't.

Finally, a nurse calls us back, and we follow her squeaking shoes and swaying ponytail down the hall. Then there he is: my dad in a hospital bed, surrounded by screens and tubes and looking . . . normal. He's not pale or bruised or bloody. He even smiles when he sees me.

"Hey, Drew. Pretty impressive performance back there, huh?"

When I step closer, he doesn't look so normal. Pale, gray, sort of . . . sunken.

"It scared the crap out of me."

He sighs. "Yeah, me too. Come sit down."

I sit on the chair by his bed. "What happens next?" I ask. I'm not really sure whether I mean tonight or tomorrow or everything after that.

"They want to watch me for a day or two. But not longer than that. I feel fine right now."

"Can I stay?"

I shouldn't have asked. I should have just done it. Dad looks up at the clock and smiles, but it takes some work. "No, you'd better get home. You've got a race to run, kiddo. See if Mia's mom or her grandma can drive you two to the starting line, and your mom can come watch you finish."

I stare at him. "You're kidding, right?"

He's not.

"Why?" I ask.

"Because it's what we've been working for all summer. This disease gets to stop me sometimes, but it doesn't get to stop you. Not ever." He blinks and clears his throat. "Promise me you'll run tomorrow. You and Mia both."

It's a pretty dirty trick to ask somebody to promise you something when you're lying in a hospital bed. What am I supposed to say?

"I don't know if I can."

He shakes his head. "Nah, that's not true. We both know you can."

He's right. Of course he's right.

"Okay, now listen to your coach. Most of the race is on stretches of the trail we've been running all summer.

All you do is run down the coast six and a half miles, then turn around and come back." I know this already, but it's still good to hear it from him. "You and Mia stick together and don't go all out on the first few miles. You need to have enough in the tank to finish. Drink at every aid station. Walk a little if you need to. And for goodness' sake, go to the bathroom if you need to. Better than a Code Brown."

"Gross! Dad!"

He puts his hands out. "I'm just saying! Don't ignore the signs your body's giving you."

We're both quiet for a second after that.

I look up at the ceiling. My voice is almost a whisper. "I don't know if I can do it without you."

Dad grips my shoulder so I'll look him in the eye.

"You have to promise me one more thing." I can't even tell him he's not playing fair, because he looks like his heart might burst any second. "Promise you won't ever stop yourself from living your best life just because I'm not there."

And dang it, gravity gets my tears and I'm crying, and then he's crying, and then Mom's crying, and I'm not sure why because this isn't the end. He'll be home in a day or two.

"I promise." It comes out so soft, but he finds my hand and squeezes hard.

He hears me.

He knows.

Mom drives me home, then goes back to the hospital to be with Dad. I maybe sleep. Or maybe not. It feels like a hundred years or five seconds before my alarm goes off. I don't have to change because I always run in the clothes I slept in. Not mixing it up now.

It's weird waking up with my parents gone and Aunt Shannon asleep on the inflatable mattress in Luna's room. But I get a little comfort from the sameness of my breakfast: some cereal and milk, a banana, and just a few swallows of water. Still, my stomach feels tight and my mouth is dry as sawdust.

I rub Scout's head for good luck and go outside to wait on the front porch. The concrete is cold through my socks until I slide on the Nikes that sort of started this whole thing. They're dirty and scuffed now, and the soles are getting a little thin. But they are hands-down my favorite shoes ever.

Our race packets came with safety pins to fasten our numbers on, which should be easy (and safe) enough. But somehow I still poke myself three times. Right as I'm pinning the last one, a car coasts up to the curb with Mia's grandma at the wheel, and Mia waves to me from the back window.

"Any news on your dad?" she asks as I climb in the back seat next to her and buckle up.

"Not this morning," I say. "But last night they said

he should be able to come home in a day or two." Then I remember why we got into this in the first place. "Are you ready to to race? And to, you know, talk to people?"

Mia bites her bottom lip. "I have to be, right? I mean, I'm nervous, but maybe I would be anyway. Are you nervous?"

I take the question and turn it over in my mind. "Not really. It's just running, right? Just one foot in front of the other, and then you stop. And maybe you talk to some other runners along the way. Right?"

"Right," she says. "That's all we're doing."

We both spend the rest of the ride trying to believe that.

The closer we get, the more crowded the streets become. Mia's grandma has to let us off a couple of blocks away, and I wonder if I'll be regretting every one of these pre-race steps when I'm struggling toward 13.1 miles.

The starting line is hard to find, partly because everywhere I look, I see lines. There are lines of blue porta-potties and lines to use the porta-potties and lines of friends having their pictures taken together. There's one straight white line down the center of the path that we'll follow the whole race—and that line eventually leads us to the starting line, where runners are already gathering. But even with all the lines, the whole thing feels like a scrambled mess. Part of me wants to hold on to Mia just so I don't get swallowed up.

Then, in the sea of unfamiliar faces, somebody surfaces right next to me who I actually recognize: Amarante, Dad's right-hand man from the shop.

"You run this every year," I remember.

He nods. "Hey, I heard about your dad. Tell him not to even think about work. Tony and I will take care of all the open jobs and work on getting the shop ready."

"I'll tell him," I say. A little of my worry washes away, maybe because Amarante is one of the only people in the world who can actually do something to help my family right now.

"You're a great kid, Drew," he says. "Good luck out there. I'd cheer for you at the finish, but I've seen you guys running. You're probably faster than I am."

I don't answer him, though, because my mind's rewinding to something he just said. He turns to walk away just as I figure out what to ask: "Ready for what?"

Amarante looks back over his shoulder. "What?"

"You said you'll take care of all the open jobs and get the shop ready. Ready for what?" I try to swallow, but my throat's too dry. "Did you mean ready to sell?"

He's uncomfortable, and I'm sorry about that, but I have to know.

"You should probably ask your dad about this," he says, which is an answer even if he doesn't mean for it to be.

"He doesn't have to sell it," I say. "I'll be ready to run

it as soon as I graduate. Can't you help us out until then?" Three generations that shop has been in my family.

Amarante smiles, but he's not laughing at me. "You don't want to run it, Drew."

"You don't know that. Even I don't know that." I think back on all the time I've spent in the shop this summer, and suddenly, I can't imagine working anywhere else. "I mean, I do know. I want to run the shop." I can't be the one who messes this up, just because Dad gave me the wrong name. Just because I thought I didn't want to work there doesn't mean I can't change. Everything can change. Obviously.

"Maybe he won't even have to sell," Amarante says. "Either way, it'll work out."

I don't believe him. I'm trying not to freak out, but Dad is not okay and there are so many things you can't do if your body is shutting down. If you might collapse any second. You can't use the tools or carry the lumber or even drive your kid to pick up his friend like Dad did just last night.

If Mom has to quit her job to take care of him, how will we pay our bills?

How are we going to pay for any of this without selling the shop?

And if we sell the shop, where will we live?

Will we be shopless *and* homeless?

"Breathe," Mia reminds me. She takes my elbow and brings me to the starting line. I'm already doing my in two, out two breathing, but it's not helping.

"I don't think I can do this," I tell her.

"Breathe," she says again. "One foot in front of the other until we get back here, and then we'll stop."

I look around for Amarante, but he's already lost in the crowd. There are hundreds of people on both sides of the path getting ready to cheer for the runners. And I don't know a single one of them.

"Don't let go," I tell Mia. "Don't lose me."

"I won't," she says.

And then the starting gun goes off.

And we are running.

In two, out two.

Because sometimes all you can do is take the next step.

And keep breathing.

18
MIA

THE FIRST HALF

I meant it when I told Drew
we wouldn't lose each other.
We've run side by side all summer
and I'm not going to stop now.

Luckily, I should still be able
to find Lucas Martin,
since the race is one big

out

and

back,

which is perfect if you're looking for somebody.

It means I'll see
> all the people who are faster than me on their way back,
> and all the people who are slower than me on *my* way back.

(Unless they cheat
and turn back early,
which seems like the kind of thing
Lucas Martin might do.)

But he doesn't cheat—
at least not when it comes to this race.
I'm barely to the turnaround point when I see him.
He's been right behind me the whole time.

The guy I've been chasing for weeks
has been chasing me for miles.

But there are
> no cameras
> and no crowd,
so maybe
> no accountability.

Doesn't matter,
I tell myself.
I'm here now,
and I didn't come all this way
just to back down.
There are good things coming
as long as you have hope.

Drew, I say.
I see him.
I see Lucas Martin.

Drew drops his voice.
Are you ready?
Do you want me to stay with you?

I shake my head.
Keep your momentum.
I'll catch up.
The fact that we've been ahead of Martin
this whole time
gives me a burst of confidence.

Drew nods and keeps the pace.
I'll try not to get too far ahead,
and I'll look for you at the aid stations.

Okay, I say, then slow to a walk for a few steps,
hoping hoping hoping
I won't miss Lucas Martin somehow.

I picture Dad's face,
and Mom's,
and Owen's,
and Oliver's,
then practice my lines.

> *Hello, Mr. Martin.*
> *My name is Mia Fisher*
> *and I want to talk to you*
> *about the house on McCallister.*

But these words,
the ones I've said over and over are
suddenly too much
and not enough
and just
all
wrong.

When he passes me,
I decide to stay right behind him for a while.

I notice
> how much he sweats,
> how his shoulders barely sway,
> how new and expensive his gear looks,
> and I wonder if he bought it all
> with money he owes other people.

What kind of person doesn't pay their bills
when they already have more than they need?
What kind of person takes another family's home?
And is there even anything he could do to stop it now?

Or is it too late?

I'm still trying to find
> new words,
> better words,
> the *right* words
when Lucas Martin runs straight up to an aid station,
takes a drink from the volunteer,
and for a second,
they talk.

He's gone by the time I get there,
but the same volunteer
turns her warm smile on me
as she hands me a cup.

Go on, she says. *You got this.*

Whether it's the drink
or something else,
I feel stronger than I did
just a few seconds ago.
And I believe her.

If she can talk to Lucas Martin,
then I can too.

But first I have to catch him.

MILE 7

Lucas Martin runs with a
swagger
that says he knows exactly what he's doing.
There's so much strength in his stride
he'll probably keep this pace
all the way to the finish line.

No, he'll probably speed up
and pick off as many poor, tired stragglers
as he can.

If I want to talk to him,
it has to be now.

So I beg my legs to go
       just a little faster
and my lungs to draw breath
       just a little deeper.

I pull my shoulders
back like a bow
ready to shoot my questions,
my truth,
straight through him.

When I'm close enough,
I reach out and touch his arm.

We both jump a little
from the shock of it.

He gives me the same wide, white-toothed smile
I know from his
worksite
and
website.

>   *Good job, kid.*

I nod at the logo on his shirt.
You a builder?

>   *Yup. If you were from Sacramento,*
>   *you might have seen my signs.*

Yeah, I might have.
It's the perfect chance
to say the words
I've been trying to say to him for months,
but they won't come out.

I think of the friendly woman at the aid station,
try to ease into the conversation
even though nothing about today
is easy.

So, Kings or Warriors?

> *Definitely Warriors.*
> *I bring my boys down for the games*
> *sometimes.*

Oh, cool. Ever meet any of the players?

> *I got Curry to sign a ball for my oldest*
> *a few years back.*

Yeah, I know. I saw your post.
I swallow those words, say,
Wow, that's lucky.
It takes a few paces
before I can get the next part out.
I bet they love spending time with their dad.

He lengthens his stride a little.
Yeah, we're pretty tight.

I breathe,
breathe,
breathe,
drawing in
all the courage I can.

Can I tell you about my dad?

He looks at me.
Um, sure.

He's a builder too.
A framer.
He helps make homes for families,
            just
            like
            you.

He looks over at me,
and his face has fallen,
like he's too tired to play an angle.
Honestly, kid, all I do is manage projects.
Guys like your dad
are the ones who actually
create something.

I hate that,
for a second,
I don't hate him.

We close in on the eight-mile marker,
and he looks down at his watch,
probably checking his pace.

I try to bring him back.
My dad was building a house for us,
but now we're going to lose it.

> *I'm sorry.*
> *I bet he'll build you a new one.*

He would if he could.

Lucas Martin is still
watching his watch.
I'm losing him.

I have to try something else,
to get the words out somehow.
Does framing pay pretty well
in Sacramento?

He's barely listening.

I guess so.

Hey, I've got to speed up to stay on pace.

I'm trying to beat my time from last year.

Keep going though, okay?

See you at the finish line?

He doesn't wait for an answer,

just

pulls

away.

And no matter how hard I push,
I can't stay with him.

I am going as fast as I can,
but I am still
losing ground
as he ramps up his pace,
passing runners
one
by
one.

I was so proud to have been
faster in the first half
that I misread his strategy.

The only strategy I have is
one foot in front of the other,
which seems so simple
and embarrassing
to think about now.

How did I ever think
I could keep up
or come out ahead?

MILE 8

Lucas Martin passes Drew at the base of a long, uphill slope.
Soon, I reach Drew too
and I know now
if I'm going to do this,
I'm going to need his help.

Hey, I say to Drew.
I talked to Lucas Martin, sort of.
Let's see if we can keep up with him.

> Drew's breathing harder than usual.
> His shoulders sag as he looks up at the hill ahead of us.
> *You go for it.*
> *I'm just trying to finish this thing.*

Then I remember
>> Pete.
I remember
>> running this race is about my friend,
>> not just my enemy.

I have to choose:
>Try to keep pace with Martin
>or
>be here for Drew.

I match my tired stride to Drew's.

You're doing great, I tell him.
Only a few more miles.
And the slower we are this year,
the easier it will be
to beat our time
next year.

>Drew loses momentum as the trail rises.
>*Unless you're my dad.*
>*This whole running thing was his idea,*
>*but he won't be able to run it next year.*
>*Or ever.*

You don't know that, I insist.
Maybe his disease will progress slowly.
Or maybe they got it wrong.
Maybe he's got some other disease
that turns itself around.
Or maybe they'll find a cure.

You think?
Drew looks at me
with so much hope
I wonder if I should take it back.

I'm not an expert or anything, I say,
but the doctors here thought Gram
had stomach cancer last year.
She's the one who finally figured out
it was just a diet thing.

Drew's pace picks up a notch.
Stephen Hawking lived with ALS
for fifty years.
And his life was pretty incredible.

Exactly, I say,
even though I'm not sure
who that is.
The only thing you have to do right now
is give this race
everything you've got.
Do you know how proud he'll be
when you cross that finish line?

Pretty freaking proud,
he says.

I imagine it then.
How proud Pete will be.

Will I make my dad proud today too?

MILE 9

At the top of the hill,
our momentum has shifted.
Now it's Drew pushing forward
and me who feels like it will take
everything I've got
just to finish this thing.

What am I doing here?

My legs are spaghetti
seasoned by the patches of salt
left behind where pools of sweat evaporated.

How did I believe I could fix anything?

My body begs me to lie down
in the rough grass
at the side of the trail
and just
sleep awhile.

How did I even think I could finish this?

MILE 10

Just after the next aid station,
I see the marker.
Ten miles was the farthest we ever trained.

Maybe it's my imagination,
but it feels like my body knows this,
wants to shut down.

My steps seem to beat a new rhythm now,
my own feet telling me
            I can't,

                      I can't,

                                I can't.

19
DREW

As we finish our tenth mile, I keep thinking about what Mia said, about cures and wrong diagnoses. I picture Dad standing with the scattered folks at the sidelines, cheering and stepping in to run beside us for a bit. Maybe it's a stretch, even in Drew's Dreamland, but I imagine him running this race with me next year. Maybe it's just that I want to believe—*need* to believe—but in this moment, it all seems possible. I get so caught up in the details of my daydream—the cringy jokes, the funny stories, dumping water on ourselves at the aid stations—that it takes me a minute to realize I'm leaving Mia behind in real life.

"Hey. Mia." I drop back to bump her forward with my elbow. "I don't want to beat you yet."

"It's okay," she says, breathing harder than I've ever heard her. She blinks fast. Looks down at the trail and slows to a shuffle. "Go ahead. You shouldn't have to be the strong one. Not today."

The strong one. I like the sound of that. And I like the thought that maybe I *am* strong—but not if it means leaving Mia behind. Not after all the miles we've run together.

"Hey," I say. "We just finished ten miles. Think about that for a second. Every step we take now, it's the farthest we've ever run."

I jog ahead of her.

"This is the farthest we've ever run."

I feel a goofy grin on my face as I dash ahead again, like maybe if I smile hard enough, she'll smile too.

"Now *this* is the farthest we've ever run." It reminds me of our first run together, when each of us was determined to go just a little farther than the other past the pier.

Only this time, Mia doesn't look like she can go even just a little farther.

So I let her catch up. "I'm about to tell you something important." I look around, lean over, whisper, like that first day in math.

"My dad is right. You and me? Our bodies are amazing. You never know what you can do until you actually do it. And we, my friend, can run 13.1 miles."

20
MIA

MILE 11

My feet still beat the rhythm:
        I can't,
                I can't,
                        I can't.

But then I look at my friend
who needs to believe
        in impossible things,
        in the power of regular people to beat the odds.

And I realize:
I need to believe
in those things too.

MILE 12

So I ignore
> the rough grass along the trail,
> the soft sand in the distance.

Instead, I imagine
flying over the Alaskan wilderness,
whales breaching in a distant bay,
glaciers towering over tundra,
nowhere to go but
> on,

> > on,

> > > on.

I think of what Drew just said
and make a deal with myself:
> Just run to that sign.
> That'll be the farthest you've ever run.
Then, when I get there:
> Just push to the top of that hill.
> That'll be the farthest you've ever run.

I make the bargain
again and again,
knowing the only reason it works
is because this
is what I've been running toward all along.

Pete is right.
Drew is right.
Our bodies
are amazing.

I've been noticing the difference for weeks.

All this struggling has made me
stronger than I have ever been.

Running has changed me.

MILE 13

As we reach the next rise,
something feels different.
Sounds different.

More people cheer at the sidelines.
Music dances down the trail from faraway speakers.

Then we come around the corner,
and I see the finish line.
Just cross that, I tell myself.
*That'll be the farthest you've ever run,
and that will be
enough.*

Ready? Drew asks.

I nod.
We take off.
Deep within us, there must have been
a little something more
we were saving
without realizing it.

My legs burn,
but the burning drives me forward.

I'm not even sure who finishes first,
because we're both laughing,
stumbling through the chute,
trying not to pass out or puke.

I imagined so many parts of this race
                    lining up to start with all those miles ahead of r
                    keeping up with Drew,
                        finding Lucas Martin,
that I forgot to imagine what it would feel like to finish.

It feels
AMAZING.

Drew is right.
You never know what you can do
until you do it,
and I
can run
13.1 miles.

AFTER

Drew goes to meet his mom and Luna,
but all I can think about
is finding a place to sit down.

Runners sprawl across the grass
like some epic battle scene from a movie.
I want to join them so badly
I can almost feel the cool green against my skin.

But when I cross to the shaded part of the lawn,
Lucas Martin is there,
reminding me why I'm here.

He looks so different
I almost don't recognize him.

No swagger,
no fancy fitness gadgets,
still no crews—camera or construction.
Just him,
lying in the grass with
        a baby asleep on his chest and
        a boy about my brothers' age
        trying to pull his shoes off.

He's laughing,
but he's trying to hold it in
so he doesn't wake the baby up.

I remind myself that
        this man did a terrible thing to us
        just for the money
        and it wasn't the first time
because part of me
still thinks
I need to hate him
to do what I came here to do.

But I don't hate him.

Lucas Martin looks my way.
Our eyes meet.
Right away, he sits up,
hands the baby to his wife.
He kisses her on the cheek,
says something in her ear,
and then
he's coming toward me.

As much as I wanted to catch him,
part of me wants to run away now.
But my legs tell me
not
one
more
step.

> He stops a few feet away.
> *Did you ask me about framers in*
> *Sacramento?*

I look down.
I guess that answers his question.

> *Are you Sam Fisher's daughter?*

I nod.
Mia, I say,
wondering if he's going to tell me
to leave him alone.

There's nobody around
to make him do the right thing
or even listen to me.

Except, when he looks back over at his family,
I wonder if
maybe there is.

> *Your dad does good work,* he says.
> *I'd hire him again any day.*

I stare at him.
>   Is he serious?
>   Am I supposed to be grateful?
I'm not even nervous anymore.
Too tired for anything but the truth.

He wouldn't take the job.
Especially not when
you're trying to take our house
instead of paying
the money you owe him.

Either he's been working on his acting skills
or he's actually confused.
So I spell it out for him.

The three-bedroom on McCallister.
He was building that for us.

He cringes a little,
like maybe he really didn't know.
I'm sorry, kid.
I thought it was a spec home.
You know, just one you build
to make a few bucks.
I like his work and
I heard he was in trouble,
so I thought taking it off his hands
would help us both out.

You could have paid him
for the job he did last spring.

He holds his hands up.
It's just business.
I've got a family to feed,
same as your dad.
We're both playing the same game.

He's not playing a game, I say.
He works overtime, trying to
            make payments,
not
            weasel out of them.

He looks straight at me,
like he really does need me to understand.
Look, I didn't know that house on
McCallister
was for your family.
I really am sorry.

Then fix it, I say,
loud enough that
the runners around us look over.
If you're so sorry, then fix it.
Pay him for the work he did.
Or give the money straight to the bank
so we can keep our house.
Your kids have a home of their own.
My family deserves that too.

His wife comes over,
one kid on her hip,
the other holding her hand.
Is everything okay? she asks.

Yeah, he says,

at the same time I say,

No,

and that
pretty much sums it up.

He swings the bigger boy
onto his shoulders,
and I look straight into the kid's eyes.
Your dad's strong, huh?

The boy nods,
smiles,
hair sticking up,
one tooth missing.

My dad's strong too, I tell him.
*Strong
and smart
and good.
He builds houses.
When I grow up,
I want to be just like him.
I bet you want to grow up
to be just like your dad.
And I bet you will.*

Then I walk away
so Lucas Martin
can't walk away
first.

SALT AND HONEY

Over by the parking lot,
I find my own patch of grass
and lie down, wondering
how long before my family
finds me in the crowd.

Mom and Gram
never knew why
I was running this race.

I'm not sure I understand it myself anymore.
Even if Lucas Martin
has some huge change of heart,
will we be able to make the payments?

I scrape a patch of salt from my neck,
another part of me turned gritty and raw
over those thirteen miles.
It's hard to imagine feeling anything but
      exhausted
      filthy
      thirsty
      empty
ever again.

Then something brushes against my fingers.
Cool and gentle and rough
and wet enough
I can feel my skin coming clean.

Scout.

I wrap one arm around her neck
and bury my face in her fur.
It's all a mess, I tell her,
and I can't fix it.
Not by myself.

I close my eyes,
give in to my body's
giving up.

Then I feel a hand on my shoulder.
                    Mia, honey.
It's Mom's voice,
but when I open my eyes, I see
they are all here for me.

Mom and Gram,
stretching out their hands to help me up.
Owen and Oliver,
ready to tackle me right back down.

And Drew.

The one who ran beside me
every mile.

21
DREW

Our bodies might be amazing, but after 13.1 miles, the high from mile 11 is long gone, and my body is *done*. I lie on the grass and wonder: How sore will my legs be tomorrow if they're already this sore now?

Because bodies are tricky too. They can make you think you're pretty much okay when you're doing the thing—running or swimming or shooting threes or whatever. They hide the truth until you're done. Until you're resting and you can handle the hurt.

I think that's how I survived the race. Not just musclewise, but Dad-wise too. I really did run it for him, but mostly I had to not think about him at all, because thinking of him made me want to sit on the side of the trail and wait for the first-aid truck.

But I'm thinking about him now. Wondering how much he's hurting and how soon he'll be able to come home. And after that, how soon he'll have to go back to the hospital.

I'm resting in the shade, letting the cool grass pull heat from my body, when something slides against my chest. Then I remember: when I crossed the finish line, someone hung a medal around my neck.

I take it out to check it out. A ribbon—thick, slick, and colorful—cuts through a silver circle the size of a sugar cookie and ten times as heavy. Way better than any prize I've won in sports before, so I must have done something amazing. Was I first place in my age division? Fastest kid overall? Man, will that make Dad proud.

I turn the medal over, and there's one big bold word cutting across the back:

FINISHER.

Well. That's disappointing. The guy who comes in dead last will be wearing the same medal as me.

So much for amazing.

When Mom and Luna come over, I hold the medal up. Luna claps her hands and sits on my stomach. She takes the medal and bites it like it really is a cookie. Mom laughs, but there's not much energy in it. "Lie there as long as you need to, Drew, and then we'll head home," she says.

I shade my eyes and look up at her. "Don't we need to get back to the hospital?"

"Honey, you've got to shower first. I love you, but you're a health hazard right now." She sits beside me in the grass and pulls Luna onto her lap. "Dad told me we should take our time, as long as we remember every detail."

There's only one way I know to do that. "Do you have a pencil? Pen? Marker? Anything?"

Mom digs around in her purse while I unpin my race number and lean back against a tree. The race number is slicker than my sketch pad, but Mom finds a super thin Sharpie that works fine. In just a few lines, I'm forming the crowd, then the finish line, then the hint of the ocean in the distance.

When I'm satisfied with the sketch, I cap the Sharpie and go off to find Scout and Mia lying in their own patch of grass. Mia seems as stiff as I am, but she gets up and talks to me for a minute. "Say hi to your dad for me," she says. "And tell him thanks. We couldn't have done this without him, and I'm glad we did it, even if it didn't go quite how we planned."

She sounds sad, and I'm not sure why until I look where she's looking.

"Holy cheese nuggets," I say. "I forgot about Lucas Martin. How did it go?"

She shrugs. "I don't think it did any good."

Well, that stinks worse than my racing clothes. I have no idea what to say, so I just stand there for a second. My brain reminds me that I am not the smoothest with girls, but my heart tells me, *This isn't a girl, this is Mia, and she is tired and torn-up just like you.*

"I'm sorry. And I'm here," I say as I open my arms, and she steps into them and hugs me back hard, even though we're both crusted with sweat.

"There are good things coming, right?" she says. "As long as we have hope?"

"You'd better believe it," I say.

It's hard to get out of the shower. There's something so satisfying about washing all that crust and sweat off. I guess it feels good to fix a problem that's totally fixable.

Mom knocks on the bathroom door. "Finish up, okay? We should get going soon."

I can do that because I am a FINISHER.

Dad would have laughed at that joke.

Am I still allowed to make jokes, though? I stuff my medal in my pocket and wonder all the way to the hospital.

This time, we go straight to Dad's room. As soon as he sees us, he sits up, looking even more like his regular self than last night. He pulls me and Luna in with one strong arm each. She curls up and turns away from him, and he gets the hint and starts scratching her back. His eyes are on me, though.

"Tell me about the race," he says. "Tell me everything."

So I do. I tell him about the crowds and crusty sweat. How good it felt to pour water over my face and down my back at the aid stations. I tell him how tough Mia was and how I saw Amarante at the starting line, even if I don't tell him what we talked about.

By then, Luna is done being still. She hops down from

the bed and starts bouncing around the room. Dad leans back against his pile of pillows. "Tell me this: How do you feel, knowing you did something you never thought you could do?"

"Sore," I say. "Holy cheese nuggets, my whole body is screaming at me. I mean, I knew my legs would be sore, but my back? My armpits? What the heck?"

He laughs, but there's something underneath it. He probably hurts all over too. And here I am, complaining like a jerk, when my body's sore because of the things it can do and his is sore because of the things it can't. When mine will be better in a day or a week and his . . . well, I don't really want to think about that.

Then a smile sneaks onto Dad's face. "Look," he says.

Luna's holding a foam ball she dug out of Mom's bag, eyeing the little metal sink. She takes the ball in both hands and shoots it out, straight from her chest. The ball hits the bottom of the cabinet and ricochets off the wall before it settles in the sink. She jumps up with her arms in the air. "Downtown!" she shouts.

Mom gets the ball out and hands it back, and Luna shoots again and again.

"Hey," Dad says. "Do we still have that plastic hoop we gave you for your birthday, way back when?"

I try to remember. "I think it's in the storage shed."

"Want to help me teach her to shoot?" he asks.

"Yeah," I say, and I mean it. I'm a decent shooter, and that sounds fun.

But when I watch Luna, my brain fast-forwards to when she'll be big enough to play for real. Shooting won't be enough. She'll need rebounding and defense and ball handling and all the stuff I'm still not that great at. What if Mom and I are all she's got? And what about all the stuff I don't even know I don't know?

There's no way I'll ever be enough without him.

"Hey," Dad says, nudging me out of my worry. "Mom says you won a medal."

"I don't know if 'won' is the right word . . ." I take it out of my pocket and hand it to him, hoping he won't be too disappointed.

"Wow." Dad nods. "That's some serious hardware."

"Yeah, but look what it says."

"'Half Moon Bay Half Marathon,'" he reads. "I like it."

"No, Dad. Look on the back."

"'Finisher,'" he reads. "Ah, that's got to feel good."

I stare. Is he messing with me?

"They gave those to everybody! The guy who came in last got the exact same medal." How does he not get this?

"Can you imagine," he asks, "how much courage it would take to come in last? How much guts you've got to have to watch everybody leave you behind and just keep going?" He traces his fingers over the letters. "Man, I wish it could've been me."

I grit my teeth. When will I stop saying the wrong things? When will I stop making this worse?

Dad hands the medal back. "I didn't mean to make

you feel bad." He lifts my chin, and the muscles in my jaw relax a little. "I don't have a fancy medal like you, but I'm a Finisher too, Drew. We're going to fight this together, and we are not giving up. Not ever."

He's right. Of course he's right. The medal feels heavier in my hands now, but I remind myself this summer has made me strong. I'll be as strong as he needs me to be. I slide my thumb along the thick ribbon as my muscles remember every single step it took to earn it. Now I want to keep the medal—polish it, frame it, wear it to school, all of the above. Now I want the whole world to know that I'm a Finisher, because that's what Dad taught me to be.

That's when I know what to do with it. I take the medal and hold it out. Dad bows his head, and I hang it around his neck.

"I'm a Finisher."

"You're a Finisher."

We say it at the exact same time.

"I have something else for you," I tell him. I grab the sketch I made on the back of my race number and hand it over.

Dad looks at it for a long time, then looks up at me with tears in his eyes. "I sure am glad I named you Drew," he says.

22
MIA

MIGRATION

This year, it feels like summer leaves
      a
             little
                      at
                         a
                                time.

Like each flock of birds
takes a piece of it with them
as they fly south.

Five days after
my own thirteen-mile migration
                                        down the coast
                      and back again,
the ache in my muscles has eased.
I can almost play tag with the twins,
and I'm not bracing myself
every time I have to climb into the car.

But still,
when Mom finds me the day before my birthday,
asks me if I want to go for a long drive,
I don't even have to think about the answer.

No thanks.

           She smiles, but it's a sad one.
           You might want to find out where I'm headed first.
           I have to go back to Sacramento
           to sign some final paperwork on the house.
           I thought we could walk through
           one last time,
           if you wanted.

I don't want to.
But I have to.
My heart tells me this,
calls me home,
even though I am weary and wondering
when I will be home to stay.

I watch the birds out my window as we drive,
wondering if this is how they feel too.

My phone buzzes with a message from Dad:
a picture of the house in Yakutat
with the orange roof
and the words *All fixed up!*

Before I can figure out
how I feel
or how to answer,
another picture comes in,
of Aunt Penny standing
in front of an enormous stove
with a gray-haired woman
who is not Grandma Jo.
*And Aunt Penny found the perfect partner
to help run the café!*

Doesn't he know what we're losing today?
Doesn't he care that not everything
is working out perfectly here?
Do we even know how
to talk to each other anymore?

For the first time all summer,
I wish he hadn't texted at all.

THE ROAD HOME

For two hours,
my conversation with Mom is like the drive:
quick
then slow
and sometimes winding,
but always with

                                              the house
                              in the distance
                      and only
            getting
closer.

It's hard to talk about it,
so we don't,
until we turn the corner
and it's right in front of us.

The house Dad was building,
we were building,
is wrecked.

WOUNDS

I don't know what I expected,
but it wasn't this.

Walls tagged with spray paint.
Two windows broken,
one just gone.

Inside, garbage scattered,
drinks spilled in every room,
a terrible smell coming from deep inside.

Holes gaping like wounds in the Sheetrock.

> Dad built the walls,
> set the windows,
> hung the Sheetrock,
> so
> it feels like it's him
> they've wounded.

Mom, I whisper. *What happened?*

> She stands perfectly still,
> soaking it all in.
> *Nobody was here to take care of it.*

It looked abandoned.
It was *abandoned.*
She reaches up,
rests a hand on the wall
like she wants to heal it.

All summer, I'd imagined our house
waiting here
just like we'd left it.
But you can't really expect that
when you've been gone for months.

In the piano alcove,
I push a corner of Sheetrock
back against the stud,
but it bows out again.

Even if we can't live in this house,
I'd rather someone else be happy here
than have it like this.

It can be fixed, I say. *Can't it?*

Of course, she says.
It will be a beautiful home for a family,
probably before the weather turns.

ELAINE VICKERS

I trace a gash in the subfloor
where the carpet will go
with the toe of my running shoe,
pushing the next words past my tongue
because none of us
have been talking to Dad as much lately,
and I have to know the answer.

Have to know if,
        like the house,
        and my sore legs,
my other aches can be healed someday too.

What if he's been gone too long
and it's different when he gets back?

RECAPITULATION

Mom sits
right in the middle of the floor,
pats the space next to her.

Holds her phone out to me as I sit beside her.
She's found the video of my first birthday—
the one where Dad surprises her
by playing the violin.

> *You've seen this, haven't you?*

I nod.
We watch together
and Grandma Jo is there,
her face lit up with music and mischief
as Dad pretends to stumble through
his simple song.

The relatives all laugh,
and Dad asks Mom
to give him another chance.
Right then—
            right before he begins to play for real—
she pauses the video.

Did he ever tell you
how long it had been
since he'd last played?
Before this video was taken?

I shake my head.

Since he was a teenager, she says.
He gave the violin to Grandma Jo and Aunt Penny
when he came to California for college.
And then ten years later,
he picked it up
and played
this.

She pushes play,
and Dad's music fills the house.

Some things are so much a part of you,
she says,
and they run so deep
> *in your heart,*
> *in your mind,*
> *in your memory,*
that you never forget.

IMPORTANT PAPERS: PART 3

We listen to Dad's song
again and again
on the way to the bank.

Inside,
we're led to a room with
>   bare walls,
>   a long table,
>   a pile of papers.

The loan officer will be right with you,
says a receptionist dressed all in gray.

But nobody comes for a long time.
I take an extra pen
from the cup in the center of the table
and start to sketch our house—
>   not the way it looked today,
>   but the way I imagined it
>   when Dad and I stood in the dirt together
>   and dreamed of living there.

I think back to the way Drew draws
and keep my pen moving and my lines loose.

(Maybe I'll even show him my drawing
when we celebrate our birthdays together tomorrow
since it's much better than the terrible drawing
I did of him.)

Finally, another woman walks in and sits across from us.
The streak of blue in her hair
matches the lines of my drawing.
On another day,
this would have made me smile.

Sorry to keep you waiting, she says,
swapping out the stack of papers on the table
for another she's just brought in.

But she doesn't seem sorry.
She seems . . . happy.
There have been some last-minute changes,
so I had to reprint everything.

Changes? Mom asks, suspicious.
What kind of changes?

She reaches for one handwritten page
on top of the stack of papers,
and I watch as her eyes go round as lemons.

Mia, she whispers.
The loan is almost paid off.
The house is still ours.
Without looking up,
she reaches out her hand,
and I slide my fingers between hers and
squeeze.

The blue-haired woman looks straight at Mom,
still smiling.
I can tell you know what you're looking at there.
Do you understand and agree to the new terms?
Are you ready to sign?

Mom's almost crying now,
but she's laughing too.
Yes, the new terms will work just fine.

HOMECOMING

Out in the parking lot,
Mom stands under a tree
holding the stack of papers with one hand,
pulling me close with the other.

What happened? I ask.

> Mom puts a hand to her mouth
> and breathes,
> breathes,
> breathes.
>
> *There was a letter from Lucas Martin*
> *in with all the paperwork.*
> *Apparently, he made*
> *a substantial payment on our loan.*
> *He said he's squaring a debt*
> *and making sure*
> *some of the good your dad has done in the city*
> *finds its way back to him.*

I bite my bottom lip,
barely able to imagine
what this might mean.
Did I make this happen?

It feels like maybe I did,
but I'm not even sure it matters.

> Mom kisses the top of my head.
> *It'll take a few weeks*
> *to finish up the paperwork,*
> *and the house itself.*
> *We'll have to come up with the money*
> *for the last finishes and fixtures.*
> *Things will be tight, even with a smaller bank paym*
> *But still, it feels like*
> *all our prayers*
> *are being answered at once.*

I squeeze her tighter and breathe in her scent—
> sea and citrus,
> like my first days in Half Moon Bay.

Wait, I say, pulling back.
What do you mean
all our prayers are being answered
at once?

> She freezes for a second,
> eyes wide.
> *I'm terrible at keeping secrets, aren't I?*

She looks so trapped that I laugh,
and then she's laughing too—
        that clear, true,
        Christmas-bells laugh
        that's been missing all summer.

            I promised I wouldn't tell, she says.
            But there's another surprise,
            even better than this one.

I think back to the texts and pictures
Dad sent this morning
and realize
what he was trying to tell me.
What it means
that the Yakutat house is all fixed up
and Aunt Penny has help for the café.

I barely dare to ask,
but I have to know.
A surprise from Alaska?

            She doesn't say a word,
            but her smile
            is answer enough.

She really is terrible at keeping secrets.

When? I ask,
hoping I know the answer.

There are tears in her eyes now.
Tomorrow.

23
DREW

The sun is setting on what's supposed to be the best day of the year. I'm sitting on the beach, sketching the water, and all I can think about is how fast the summer went by. Even if it wasn't the greatest ever (and even though we've been back in school a few weeks already), I'm not ready for it to be over. How can one summer be enough time for everything to go wrong, but not enough time to fix anything?

Dad walks along the beach. He tosses a foam football to Scout like he doesn't have a care in the world, but if you look closely, he's wearing a foot brace now. And someday, the brace won't be enough. Someday he'll fall again.

On the outside, though, it doesn't seem so different from all my other birthdays. But it should be. Mia said we'd celebrate our birthdays together, but then she missed school yesterday. And when I texted her this morning, she didn't answer.

My phone buzzes in my pocket, and I wonder if it's her.

But it's Isaac calling.

"Did you get my present in the mail?" he asks. "Are you ready to open it?"

"Yes and yes," I say, rummaging through one of the big tote bags Mom brought.

"Switch to a video call," he says, and Mom takes the phone and switches the mode so Isaac can watch me and I can have my hands free to open the present. I'm not sure why we're making such a big deal out of this until I open the wrapping and HOLY CHEESE NUGGETS IT'S THE TIME CAPSULE.

"Holy cheese nuggets," I say. "It's the time capsule! Where did you find it?"

Isaac laughs. "We didn't bury it in the cypress grove at all. Remember? The trees all looked the same, so we decided I should take it home and bury it in the sandbox in my backyard."

I stare at him. "That's right! But . . . you don't live in that house anymore."

"If you're asking whether I snuck into the backyard of my old house and dug this up with some other kid's shovel, the answer is . . . maybe."

I can't stop laughing. "We have the worst memories ever. Do you even remember what's inside?"

"Yup," he says. "And you will too, as soon as you see it."

The Scotch-tape seal is still all around the box, so I know Isaac hasn't opened it yet. He really does remember, clear back from last year. I started out this summer so worried that he was going to forget me or move on without me, but he hasn't. He's holding on even better than I am.

Some of the tape crackles apart in my hands as I peel it back, but I just keep going until the box is open to reveal . . .

"Holy cheese nuggets," I say again. (It's that kind of day.) "It's Repair Guy! My brain has been trying to remind me about this all summer."

Repair Guy is the greatest comic in the history of comics. Or, it would be if we'd ever finished it. One summer, Isaac and I decided to be like the *Dog Man* kids and make our own comic series. Isaac would write the stories and I'd draw the pictures. *That* was our recipe for the greatest summer ever: We were going to find a way to publish *Repair Guy* and become very rich and very famous.

But now it's pretty obvious that Isaac and I had different . . . artistic visions. I wanted to make the comic funny and snappy and basically a rip-off of *Dog Man*. Isaac wanted it to be more serious and have Repair Guy save the world with his gadgets and basically be a rip-off of Batman. What I'm actually holding in my hand is about ten pages of comic garbage, including a hero who looked suspiciously like a skinny sixth grader with curly black hair because I didn't have anybody but Isaac to look at while I worked on the pictures.

I take my phone back from Mom with one hand and flip through the pages with the other.

"I'd forgotten how terrible this was! Wow. Just . . . wow."

Isaac laughs. "Hey. It's awesome. Honestly, we made

such a great team I'm surprised we didn't get any farther than that."

"Yeah, no," I say. "This is priceless, but it's also total garbage. You're right about one thing, though: we do make a great team."

Isaac does a fake-sad sigh. "Yeah, but we didn't have a chance to finish *Repair Guy*. Or conquer *TitanIAm*."

I shrug. "Maybe next summer."

"Yeah, next summer," he says. Then, "Dude, did you fix your hair? For Mia?"

"Relax," I say. "I just went in the water, and you know my hair naturally looks this good when it's wet. Besides, we both know you're the one with a crush on Mia."

Isaac tries to shrug it off. "She's cool, I guess."

I smile at a memory. "Confession: I thought she was the Blue Lady the first time I saw her."

I've always been a sucker for ghost stories, but this is so weird even for me that he busts up laughing.

"Hey," I say. "She was wearing a blue dress." Then I shiver; the memory feels almost like a ghost when she's only been gone a day. I need to see the real Mia. Where is she?

After Isaac and I end the call, Luna comes up beside me. As usual, she's the perfect distraction. I bury her bottom half in a mound of sand, then shape her a mermaid tail with the flat edge of a shell.

"Hey," I say. "Do you want me to teach you to write your name?"

She's a little young, but she's a lot smart. She draws a solid *L* in the sand.

"Okay, let's learn the next one. You need a *U*."

I hand her a stick and help her make a straight line down. "Now scoop it back up."

"Scoop it up!" she cries, flipping sand into the air with the stick.

I point to the horizon, where a half moon is just coming up. "Did you know your name means 'moon'?"

She frowns. "Yuna's name is *Yuna*."

"Right," I say. "Should we try the *N*?"

Instead of making an *N*, Luna wriggles out of her mermaid tail and runs away. I guess learning one new letter was enough.

Then I realize where she's running—and what she's shouting.

"Mia! Mia!"

She's right. There's Mia and her brothers and grandma and mom coming down the steps.

And a guy.

A guy carrying sand buckets, wearing a UC Sacramento shirt and a huge grin. He takes Mia's mom's hand and whispers something in her ear, and this clear, joyful laugh just pours out of her. That's when I'm sure he's Mia's dad.

Mia hugs me hello and Mr. Fisher starts shaking the adults' hands, so I toss away my letter-writing stick so he can shake my hand too. Then he sets himself down in the sand with his buckets and starts to build. Pretty soon the twins and Luna become his construction crew, and the base of a sandcastle starts to take shape. Apparently, Dad knows Mia's mom from high school, because after they're done reminiscing about the day we were born, they're laughing about how she helped him out more than once with his junky truck that couldn't drive in reverse.

When it's time to eat, we load paper plates with fruit and chips and hamburgers. Then we sit in camp chairs and on beach blankets—except Luna and the twins, who run around with their parents following behind, feeding them a bite at a time. Life is just too exciting to stop and eat when you're little, I guess.

After everybody's finished with dinner, Mom brings out a huge birthday cake with icing and strawberries and two clusters of candles. Mia and I smile at each other and blow them out at exactly the same time, and it doesn't really matter whose breath blows out whose candles. We're too old now to believe that your wish won't come true because your friend helped you. In real life, it's pretty much the opposite.

I take my cake and wander back down to the water. I sit in the sand, balancing the plate on my knees as I try to hold each bite on my tongue so it will last just a little longer. Soon Mia is there too, watching the waves next to me.

"I can't believe your dad is here," I say to Mia.

She smiles. "I can't believe it either."

We look back at where Mia's dad and brothers are

building their sandcastle again. He lifts one of the twins over his head and flies him over the moat.

"He looks like a superhero," I say.

"My brother or my dad?" she asks.

"Both, I guess. Is your dad back for good?"

"Yup. The next time he goes to Alaska, he promised to take us with him."

Maybe every once in a while, something can get fixed in a summer.

Then I realize what that means. "Are you moving back to Sacramento?"

Mia stretches her fingers into the sand. "Once the house is ready. Not tomorrow or anything, but probably soon."

"So you're leaving," I say. "This is it."

"Maybe," Mia admits. "I won't live here anymore, but I'll come back to visit. Hopefully a lot, and especially in the summers." She starts scooping sand over her feet, anchoring herself in place. "I spent all summer wanting so badly to be home that I didn't even notice how much it feels like I belong here now. I thought going back to Sacramento would mean I could stop feeling split in two, but now . . ."

Mia brushes off her hands and pulls something from her pocket—the little carved bird. "It looked so perfect next to yours on the windowsill in the shop," she says. "Would you keep it there for me? It feels like they belong together."

"If that's what you want," I say, taking the bird from her and sliding it into my pocket. "That way at least I know you'll come back for it someday. Right?"

"Right," Mia says, and the way she looks me straight in the eye, I believe her.

Mia and I settle back, watching the waves roll in and out, in and out. I want to hope that if we've found our way back to each other before, it could happen again. But if I've learned anything this summer, it's that you never know when you'll be pulled from one world to another, and you sure as heck can't control it.

I decide to change the subject. "Did you bring your violin?"

"Yup." She nods at her dad. "Let's ask him to play it. It actually sounds really good."

Okay, I'm a little skeptical when the superhero castle-builder tightens the bow and sticks the violin under his chin. It looks like a toy there, to be honest. But as soon as he starts playing, everybody stops talking. The melody seems familiar, and finally, I realize what it is.

"'Half Moon Summer,'" I say. "He's playing our song!"

I pass my guitar over to Mom (who plays a lot better than I do). Pretty soon we're all singing with the crackle of the fire and the rush of the waves for percussion. They start another song after that, and there will probably be another one after that, but eventually, there will be a last song. There has to be. And then what happens?

Dad leaves his chair and comes to sit in the sand beside me. "What's wrong, Drew?"

I take a pinch of sand and roll it between my fingers. "Isaac's not here, and Mia's moving too. And you . . ." I can't even finish it, but I don't need to. He puts his arm around me.

"I'm the lucky one, to have a kid like you. Did I ever tell you about the day you were born?"

I bump my elbow against his, because yeah, of course. He tells that story every year. "I wouldn't stop crying until they put me in with her." Mia's doing a magic trick for Luna and the twins, hiding a shell in one hand and making it appear in the other, and they shriek with laughter every time. They look like they should be in a movie or something.

It's another perfect moment in a perfect night that can't last.

I close my eyes and try to sketch the picture of this night in my memory so I'll always have it with me. I feel the warm weight of Scout settling herself against my legs. She lays her head in my lap as I add her to my sketch.

Dad clears his throat and puts an arm around me. "Happy birthday, Drew."

"It's almost over," I say. I don't open my eyes. "And it might never be like this again." He doesn't argue, just holds me safe against his shoulder.

"But aren't we lucky it happened at all," he says, and he sounds a little like Lou Gehrig, almost. "What a summer."

"I wish I could go back and fix it all," I say. "Do everything better. Remember better. Just . . . be better."

"Me too. But life is like that old truck of mine. It'll take you just about anywhere you're set on going, but it doesn't go in reverse."

By the fire, they've circled around to "Half Moon Summer" again. I open my eyes, and this time I sing, because I want to make the most of this night, this song, this moment.

Even if it never happens again, it's happening now, and I feel like the luckiest kid on the face of the earth.

ACKNOWLEDGMENTS

Writing a book is a bit like a long-distance race, and I am forever grateful for those who ran by my side and cheered me on, all along the way.

The idea for this story came as I was training with my son, Jack, for our first half marathon together. It involved a fairly gruesome fall seven miles into a ten-mile training run, a speedy rescue from a dear friend, Shannon Rowley (who had gotten me into running half marathons in the first place), and a text message she sent me afterward that changed everything. Thank you, Shannon, for being the kind of friend who saves the day *and* gives you the idea for your next book.

Huge thanks to my incredible agent, Ammi-Joan Paquette, whose enthusiasm and encouragement helped this one to the finish line in so many ways.

Catherine Frank, my brilliant editor, you have been the greatest coach and trainer all along the route. Thank you for pushing me, encouraging me, and believing in me in ways that brought out the very best in this story.

Deepest thanks to everyone at Peachtree who helped turn a Word file on my computer into an actual book, including cover artist Chloe Zola, copy editor Chandra Wohleber, proofreader John Simko, and designer Lily Steele.

Thanks beyond measure go to Tara Dairman, Jennifer Chambliss Bertman, and Ann Braden—aka the Rocket Cats—who ran beside me every mile. I can't imagine anyone I'd rather be navigating this journey with than you.

Huge thanks to my other readers, who critiqued and coached and shaped this story in their own ways: Erin Shakespear Bishop, Helen Boswell-Taylor, Rosalyn Eves, Tasha Seegmiller, Amanda Rawson Hill, Cindy Baldwin, Frank Cole, Jane McCallister, Mason McCallister, Guizella Rocabado, Maria Rocabado, Catriella Freedman, Kendra Levin, Meira Drazin, Suri Rosen, Ari Goelman, Sarah Aronson, and Susan Meyer.

Thanks to Peter Glahn for the story and the imagery of the truck that doesn't run in reverse and the permission to use it here. And thank you for being the kind of educator who helps kids move forward and gives them courage and confidence for the journey.

Thank you to Jenny Call, Summer Hodson, Bridget Lee, Brooke MacNaughtan, Jane McCallister, and Robyn Orme for a trip to Half Moon Bay I'll never forget—and a million other memories that are as priceless to me as your friendship.

The deepest thanks always go to my family, who support me and cheer me on in everything from writing to teaching to running half marathons. Lucy, Halle, Jack, and Robbie, you mean the world to me.

Thank you to my grandmother Alice Braithwaite for helping me love reading and theater and life and for introducing me to *Our Town* when I was almost exactly Mia's age.

Thank you to my parents for being there for every mile, always.

And to Kenton Call and his beautiful family, whom I think about with every page of this story. What a light you shone in this world—and it shines on, even now, and always. I am eternally grateful that my story has been shaped by yours.

ABOUT THE AUTHOR

ELAINE VICKERS is an award-winning author of picture books and middle grade and young adult novels. She grew up reading, running, and exploring in a small town in Utah. Several years and one PhD later, she found her way back to her hometown, where she spends her time writing, teaching college chemistry, and exploring with her family. Visit her at *ElaineVickers.com*.